"There's a stool inside the grooming area. Let me get it." Ginnie dragged it to the hallway.

"Steady it, and let me climb." I swiveled the camera toward my face once I was high enough to reach it and felt a sticky blob covering the lens. My heart sank. Pinching off a bit, I smelled it. "Ginnie, it's bubblegum."

We checked the camera at the other end of the hallway. More gum. Frustration welled in my chest as I dropped to the floor. "Looks to me like they have been sabotaged."

She covered her mouth with one hand. "Oh no, this can't be happening." She shivered.

I gripped her arm. "Did you call Sheriff Connors?" At her nod, I guided her down the hall, heartsick. I wondered where Scholander's Pride might be—and who would have gone to such trouble to take her.

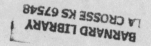

Don't miss out on any of our great mysteries. Contact us at the following address for information on our newest releases and club information:

Heartsong Presents—MYSTERIES! Readers' Service
PO Box 721
Uhrichsville, OH 44683
Web site: www.heartsongmysteries.com

Or for faster action, call 1-740-922-7280.

Dog Gone

A Feather Duster Mystery

Eileen Key

HEARTSONG
PRESENTS
MYSTERIES

Dedication:

My appreciation goes to Barbour editor Susan Downs and my agent, Tamela Hancock Murray, for believing I could write a book. Cheryl Williford, you jump-started this. My sister, Kelly Ender, primed the pump. Kim Sawyer and Margie Vawter, thanks for holding my hand and the red pens. ACFW members, you taught me so much. I appreciate the information given to me by the staff of Hill Country Animal Hospital and Palms Pet Resort, as well as by Brenda Matheny of BrenRich Newfoundlands.

No better friends exist than Caron and Lee Wise. Sarah, Rachel, Matthew, Dawn, Matt, Trevor, and Eliana—my family means the world to me. I love you.

This book is dedicated to my parents, Bill and Sue Caudel, who art in heaven. Thank You, Lord, for allowing me this adventure.

ISBN 978-1-59789-710-5

Cover design: Kirk DouPonce, DogEared Design
Cover illustration: Jody Williams

Our mission is to publish and distribute inspirational products offering exceptional value and biblical encouragement to the masses.

Printed in the U.S.A.

1

S chotzie's gone!"
My best friend, Ginnie's, panicked voice traveled through the phone like an electric shock and sent fear tingling through me. I jerked the receiver away from my ear and set my iced tea glass on the counter. "What do you mean *gone*?"

"Gone, Belle," she exclaimed. "She's disappeared!" She choked back a sob. "I've searched all over Pampered Pooch. I simply can't find her. Please. Hurry. Come help me look. Please!"

"I'll be right there. We'll scour the property. Promise." A knot tightened in my stomach. The loss of an expensive show dog wouldn't bode well for Ginnie's business. Nor me, since I held the lease on her property.

I stared at the laundry pile on the kitchen floor. Hanging up the phone, I toed a pair of dirty blue jeans in my laundry pile. The washing would simply have to wait. "Oh, Schotzie, where are you?"

I tugged my purse strap over my shoulder and rummaged for my car keys within its depths. My fingers fumbled over breath mints, a checkbook, two tubes of lipstick, and empty peppermint wrappers. I finally found the key ring wrapped around the strap on my cell phone case. I untangled the glob and headed out the back door.

Ginnie Reynolds and I had been friends through the births of our children and the losses of our spouses.

Her new Pampered Pooch doggie hotel and spa was a hit in our small bedroom community of Trennan, just outside Jackson. It offered a safe and comfortable place to leave a beloved dog while their owners traveled or worked. Or so the brochure said.

My Jeep rumbled in traffic. It needed a tune-up, but that would mean a day without a vehicle. I hated the trapped feeling. Why is it the minute you give your car to the mechanic, you think of a thousand errands you need to run?

Worry tugged at my brow. Schotzie was a particular favorite of mine. She'd been taught to respond to *setzen* and *handschlag*. She'd sit, extend a paw for a handshake, and lie down on command. But only a German command. An intelligent, bilingual pup. An expensive pup. One Ginnie couldn't afford to lose. Violet Lester had boarded Schotzie the day before yesterday to go to her mother's seventy-fifth birthday party in Little Rock. They would be gone a week. Two-year-old Schotzie was almost ready for breeding, and Violet couldn't cope with her kids, her mom, and a dog potentially in heat.

A short drive brought me to Ginnie's house, settled in the front section of the nine acres I'd leased to her for her new business venue. Situated away from the highway, the Pampered Pooch lay at the secluded end of a winding gravel road lined with kudzu-covered trees. The tenacious, deep green vine looped around anything in its way. Black shutters trimmed the windows of two redbrick houses nestled closely together. One house had been converted into a kennel for dogs, and the other was where Ginnie lived.

I parked under a huge magnolia and got out of the car. My tennis shoes crunched through the pebbles as I made my way across the drive. Ginnie appeared on the porch. Her distressed look made my stomach flutter, and I picked up my pace.

Ginnie, dressed in a size 4 lavender linen pantsuit covered by a purple vet smock, leaned against the porch railing wringing her hands. "Oh, Belle, this could put me out of business." She ran her fingers through her short, bottle-blond curls. "What will I do?"

I pulled her into a hug. "Let's start from the pen. Surely she couldn't have gone too far." I pressed my hand against Ginnie's back and steered her toward the gate in the chain-link fence on the south side of the house-turned-kennel. We crossed the dog-free exercise yard. There was no place for an animal to hide here. A bone-shaped, shallow pond sat in the center of the freshly mown grass waiting for the first group of pups to arrive. "Show me where Schotzie slept," I said, scanning the yard one more time.

Ginnie wheeled about, and I followed. We slipped through the back door into the house. "She was in suite number one."

The three-bedroom home had been reconfigured into tiny dog-sized apartments, or suites, as the brochure called them. Painted concrete floors echoed with the sharp barks of remaining patrons as we entered. The smell of kibble greeted my nose, but nothing else. Ginnie was adamant about keeping the kennel spotless. She'd fashioned every space so the floor was sealed and had its own drain to allow a daily wash.

Marble tile covered the walls, adding to the cleanliness and beauty.

Each area was decorated in a theme. A poster with a flowing field full of sheep hung on the wall of the room designated for border collies, and a boutique-style parlor hosted a wiggling poodle. But compared to the escapee Schotzie, all other boarders could be considered mutts. We rounded the corner, and Ginnie pointed at the empty space. Schotzie's suite had a German theme, of course. Ginnie felt that as a registered, trophy-winning schnauzer, Schotzie—short for Scholander's Pride—deserved the best.

I peered through the glass door at the decor. Every time I looked at this canine extravagance, I tried not to roll my eyes. A green velveteen child-sized lounging sofa, sitting on a plush pile area rug, dominated the room. Small pictures of Alpine mountains graced the cream marble back wall. Two gold-rimmed china bowls for food and water sat on a woven placemat. Chew toys and a bone were strewn about, and a rhinestone-studded leather leash hung on a clip beside the glass door. The luxury surroundings far outdid my son's childhood bedroom.

"Now, explain what happened," I said.

"I placed her in here after her walk last night." Ginnie motioned with her hands.

I nodded. "What time was that?"

She tapped her fingernail against her chin. "Let's see. About ten. When Schotzie is at home, her owner, Violet, always takes her out during the nightly news. She says Schotzie doesn't like seeing violence on television."

I'm sure I did roll my eyes then. The volatile Violet Lester and her rowdy children could likely wind up on the evening news on any given day. "Then what?"

"I hung Schotzie's leash on the hook, gave her a treat, and locked the door." Ginnie groaned. "Or I thought I locked it." She fumbled with the latch. "What if I didn't?"

I reached for the doorknob and turned it back and forth. "If you didn't lock the door, Ginnie, the dog wouldn't know. It was closed." I glanced at the latch. "She couldn't have pushed it with her nose to get out. She would've had to have help."

Ginnie paced the hallway. "I need to call Sheriff Connors. That dog's worth a fortune." She tugged a cell phone from her purple vet smock then dropped her hand to her side. "Oh, Belle, what am I going to do?"

"We'll figure it out. Call the sheriff while I take a look around outside." I started for the back door. "And you can always file insurance. That's all you can do if we can't find the dog."

Ginnie gasped. "File insurance? Of course we can do that. But what will I tell Violet Lester's daughter?" She rubbed her forehead. "This dog was Linda's life. After they won the last show, she planned to breed Schotzie for college money." Ginnie groaned again. "I'll never be able to replace the love that child had for her dog." Tears threatened to spill over her mascaraed eyelashes. "And what will this do to the kennel's reputation? Arabelle, my heart is broken."

I sighed. "I may not be much of a dog lover, but I know how much this business and these animals mean to you." A lost show dog would reflect on Ginnie's business and hit my pocketbook. The taxes on my property had jumped significantly. And if Ginnie's revenue was cut, she'd not be able to make the quarterly lease payment in June. I certainly couldn't cover it all. I'd risk losing land that had been in my family for three generations.

While Ginnie placed the phone call, I went to the back door and stepped outside. I ran my fingers lightly over the doorjamb by the knob. No sign of forced entry. No shoe prints. I circled to the front door and two windows. Nothing. A thick black wire caught my eye.

"Security cameras." I opened the door and hollered, "Ginnie, the cameras."

"What?"

"Your security cameras. Let's look at the tapes."

"Of course. They're so new I never thought of them. Where's my mind today?"

Mounted in the top corner of two hallways, black cameras gave a view of all the doggie domains. We could pull the tapes and solve our dilemma. Schotzie could be home by dinnertime.

Ginnie met me underneath a camera. "I can't believe I didn't run to them right off. This one would show more."

I braced an arm against the wall, stood on tiptoes, and peered at the camera to check its angle. It pointed toward the first row of doggie boudoirs. I couldn't see well. "Looks like something is on the lens."

"There's a stool inside the grooming area. Let me get it." Ginnie dragged it to the hallway.

"Steady it and let me climb." I swiveled the camera toward my face once I was high enough to reach it and felt a sticky blob covering the lens. My heart sank. Pinching off a bit, I smelled it. "Ginnie, it's bubblegum."

We checked the camera at the other end of the hallway. More gum. Frustration welled in my chest as I dropped to the floor. "Looks to me like these have been intentionally sabotaged."

She covered her mouth with one hand. "Oh no, this can't be happening." She shivered.

I gripped her arm. "Did you call Sheriff Connors?" At her nod, I guided her down the hall, heartsick. I wondered where Scholander's Pride might be—and who would have gone to such trouble to take her.

The sheriff's dispatcher had promised to send out a deputy to investigate, and Ginnie and I waited in the kennel's kitchen. Ginnie had purchased a glass-and-chrome dinette, a black refrigerator, and matching microwave. Pampered Pooch's lounge offered comfort to its employees, too.

"Coffee?" Ginnie motioned to the pot. "I mean tea. I know you don't drink coffee. See how scrambled my brain is?" She filled two mugs with water and placed them in the microwave. I opened a tea bag and dunked it in the cup she handed me.

"Who had access to the kennel last night?"

"Only Charlie Baker, my evening tech. He left before nine." Ginnie dipped her tea bag up and down and stared into space. "I heard him leave."

I reached for a packet of sweetener and stirred it

in. "I thought it was his job to walk the dogs."

"Well, it is, but I enjoy doing it sometimes. Keeps the lonesomes away." She batted her eyelashes and fought tears. "I hate bedtime now that Mitch is gone." Her voice strained, "Two long years of emptiness."

I squeezed her hand. "We'll figure this out, honey." I sipped tea and looked at her over the rim of the cup. "Don't fret. It makes wrinkles around your eyes." And it was giving me a pounding headache.

She fingered her eyelids and smoothed out the crow's-feet, massaging her temples. Ginnie's blond curls and perfect makeup were her trademarks. I must admit, she had a touch of vanity. Often she'd tried to get me "to spruce up a bit," as she called it, but I liked my less-than-perfect look. I could smear on foundation and a dab of lipstick and be out the door faster than she could curl her eyelashes.

A car pulled up, and Ginnie popped up to look out the window. "It's Deputy Dawg." A sad smile tugged at her lips.

Don Dawson seemed to enter the door behind his protruding belly. He'd earned his nickname with his slow drawl and droopy jowls, but for the many years I'd known him, he'd always proven to be a good friend. I tipped my teacup in his direction and hid my smile as I sipped.

He nodded in my direction. "Morning, Miss Ginnie." He slid his mirrored sunglasses into his pocket. "Coffee smells mighty good." Ginnie pointed to the cabinet, and he grabbed a Styrofoam cup. "Sheriff said to get here quick. What's the trouble?"

"I've lost a dog." Ginnie's forlorn voice sounded childlike.

He sipped his coffee. "Lost him?" He looked around the room as though Schotzie were under the table.

She crossed her arms. "I have searched the premises, Don, and the dog is simply not here."

I spoke up, "What's worse, the security cameras have been disabled." I explained the gum.

"Well, let's take a look-see." He ambled into the hallway and stopped. "Show me around this fancy place." He grinned. "I told my wife you'd opened a hotel for dogs, and she couldn't believe me. I'll get to tell her tonight I took a tour."

"Don, I'll gladly give you a tour, but you're here to help me find a dog." Ginnie practically stomped her tiny size 5 sandal. "Not just any dog, either. A dog worth thousands of dollars."

His eyebrows shot up. "Thousands?"

"Thousands," I echoed. "This is an award-winning show dog. We need to find her." I slid my chair from the table and patted Don on the back. "This way, Deputy."

We trailed behind Don. He prodded the pink gum on the camera with a pen then jotted something in a notebook. "Need to check for fingerprints," he murmured. Jiggling the door handles at each entrance brought another notation.

Outside the warm air felt good to my chilled arms. I gazed at the exercise yard and the pasture beyond, my throat tightening. No horses left to feed. Peter, my ex, hadn't liked the country.

"Belle, Don's found something."

I shook off the gloom and caught up with them. Don stood on a concrete block tipped against the back wall. He peered at the windowsill to the storage room high above my head.

"Those windows have been painted shut since I was a kid," I said.

"Not anymore. Crowbar marks. Been opened recently." He stepped down. "Need to talk to your employees, Ginnie." He wrote another note. "What else is missing?"

"I don't know. I was so upset about Schotzie—"

"Let's take a look." He cupped Ginnie's elbow and guided her inside.

Ginnie walked to her tiny office and wailed, "My laptop!"

Don nodded. "Anything else?"

She rifled through her desk and shook her head. "No," she whispered.

My stomach clenched again. "All your records are gone?"

"Actually," she said as she lifted a black box from under the desk, "the external hard drive is here, so they are backed up." She set it on the desk and covered her face with her hands. "I feel sick."

No more sick than I feel, I thought and walked into the kitchen.

Ginnie had called Charlie to come meet us, and he sat at the glass table waiting.

"Oh, Charlie." Ginnie grabbed his arm. "Schotzie's not here."

The lanky teenager's brown hair stuck up in all directions, and his shirt hung out from his jeans. He looked exhausted. His appearance concerned me. "Are you okay?"

"Morning, Miss Belle." He nodded. "Yes, ma'am, I'm just tired. I got in late from my job at the grocery."

Ginnie smiled at the teen. "He works nights after he leaves here. Trying to raise money for college. I hated to call and wake him." A frown crossed her face. "But the Lesters' dog is. . ." Tears trickled from her eyes, and she crumpled into a chair. "I'll be ruined when this news gets out."

Charlie frowned. "Miss Ginnie, what about the dog?" He slid one hand to her shoulder. "Schotzie was fine last night."

"The dog's missing. Didn't you hear the lady?" Deputy Don pulled out his notebook. "Baker, I need to know your whereabouts after you left the kennel."

All three of us gaped at him. I said, "Don, didn't you just hear Charlie? He was working at the grocery." I pointed at the boy. "Look at him."

"Doesn't account for all of his time. He might be covering up something." He leaned against the kitchen counter. "Start with when you left here. What time was it?"

Charlie recounted his movements. He'd gone straight home, he said, showered, put on a shirt with a store logo, and gone to work.

"Seems to me you could've carried a dog with you." The deputy drew up and glared at him. "Did you?"

"No sir, I didn't have any dog with me." Charlie's

lips drew a grim line.

"Anyone see you last night?"

"Well, no." Charlie scrubbed his hand over his unshaven jaw. "I mean, yeah. My mama—she was home." Charlie crossed his arms. "And she's allergic to dog hair. That's why I'm good about showering when I come in. I even wash my own clothes after being in the kennel."

"He's right about that, Don." Ginnie nodded, her blotchy face covered in mascara trails. She'd be highly embarrassed when she passed a mirror, so I handed her a napkin and pointed to her face. "His mama's told me she's allergic." She gave a reassuring smile at Charlie while swabbing her cheeks. "He's a good boy and works hard."

The deputy scowled. "I'll be sure to check your alibi, son. But run through last evening slow for me."

Charlie rubbed his hand across his jaw again. "Um, I got home, and while Mom warmed me up supper, I played a computer game." Charlie shifted in his chair. "Then after I ate, I rode my bike to the grocery store, locked it, and put groceries on the shelf all night. Not that it pays that much." His mouth twisted in a half grin.

"Working there by yourself, were you?"

"With the night store manager, Mr. Greeley's brother-in-law. He was there. And two other stockers."

Don nodded. "Okay. If I have any other questions, I'll call you." He scribbled Charlie's phone number.

Charlie stepped to the door. "I'm sorry 'bout Schotzie, Miss Ginnie."

Ginnie waved. "Thank you. You take this afternoon

off. Get some rest."

Charlie wandered outside and hopped on his bicycle without a backward glance.

Don faced Ginnie. "He chew gum much?"

"I've never noticed."

"Who has keys to the place?"

"Charlie and me. He usually locks up, but lately I've done it." Ginnie ran a hand through her hair, fluffing curls.

"Lot of trust you put in that Baker kid."

Ginnie sighed. "Don, I've known the family for years. I trust him."

"No one else works here?" Don's gaze swiveled around the room.

"Sukey and her daughter clean during the day and play with the day camp dogs." Ginnie pressed two fingers to her lips. "Oh, and Sukey has a key, too, to come and go when she has a client to groom."

Don sighed and scribbled in his notebook. "I'll have to question her, too."

"How is the day camp going?" I asked.

"Day camp?" he spit out the words.

"Yes, Don." Ginnie turned to me. "It's been great. I have six clients now who drop off their pups every other morning at nine and pick them up by six."

Don blew out a laugh. "In Trennan?"

A crease formed between her eyes. "People worry about their dogs when they leave them alone all day, and this gives the pups a chance to work off their energy and be watched."

The deputy looked at Ginnie then at me. He tossed

his cup in the trash and hitched his belt. "Well, I like my hound dog, but he ain't going to no day camp. He can sleep on the porch." He fake tipped his hat. "Ladies, I'll be leaving now. Miss Ginnie, I'll be in touch. Sheriff Connors will need to come out, too."

He turned around, hand raised. "One more thing, Miss Ginnie. Did the dog have one of those tracking devices? Saw that on TV." Don puffed out his chest. "You know, one of those computer chips?"

"Yes, she did. But those only work when you find the dog. They don't allow you to track them with a GPS system."

"Hmm. As expensive as that dog is, it should."

Ginnie walked him to the door as I nursed another cup of tea. "I never appreciated his height until today. I need to have those windows nailed shut." She huffed her way back to the kitchen and poured a cup of coffee. "Belle, I can't afford this loss." She sat beside me. "You well know that."

"It's going to work out. Don't start fretting now." I gulped down the frets in my throat.

Picking up a folder, Ginnie slid out some forms. "Look. At the day camp, we keep track of their exercise hours and diets. I've even had photos made for a bulletin board I want to put up." A pamphlet flipped out of the folder, and Ginnie bent to retrieve it. "And I'm thinking of getting webcams for the individual kennel suites. Then the moms and dads could watch their pups while they're away." She propped her elbow on the table. "It's been really successful in other markets—stepped up their enrollment. I think it will be worth the costs."

"Are you kidding me?" I reached for the information. Webcam prices made me gasp. "This is so expensive."

"People are interested in checking on their pets." She reached for the pamphlet. "Who knew this industry would grow so quickly? And it can be amazingly profitable."

"Certainly not penny-pinching me." I took a sip of tepid tea. "Have you considered who would know Schotzie was here?"

Ginnie shrugged one shoulder. "Violet leaves her here when they go out of town. I guess anyone could know." She sniffled. "I dread talking to them."

My eyes lit up. "Wouldn't the dog be insured? Like a life insurance policy?"

She touched a trembling hand to her face. "Violet let the coverage lapse. She told me about it last month. Said until Schotzie had pups, money would be tight." Ginnie folded and refolded a napkin, tears brimming in her eyes.

I nodded and glanced at my watch. "Ginnie, I've got to get to work. I'll call you before bedtime. Promise."

She gave me a forlorn look. "Thanks for driving out here."

I hugged her. "It's going to be okay. I know the Lesters, and I'll help you talk to them if you need me to."

"Oh, Belle, thank you." She squeezed my hand. "You're so diplomatic, having been a preacher's wife and all."

Little good it had done me. I smiled and dashed for

the Jeep, avoiding the sandbox area, which would soon hold romping pups. In a hurry, I waved at Sukey who was driving in. Little did she know she was a suspect in Schotzie's disappearance—at least in Deputy Dawg's mind.

My first client's house was a good thirty-minute drive back into Jackson if the traffic was right.

Diplomatic preacher's wife. Seems like another life. A wave of self-pity threatened, and I accelerated. Dwelling on the past wouldn't get my future any brighter or pay the stack of bills on my table. I had a house to clean.

2

Donetta Robins's five-bedroom home sat in the Lakeside subdivision, a new development for the upwardly mobile. Old farmland turned into expensive real estate. Location, location, location, and all. Huge homes with multicar garages dominated four-acre lots. Ancient trees had been chopped down to provide plenty of green space—the perfect size for the riding lawn mower kings.

The lake in the center of the subdivision was a dredged out pond, but it seemed to give the residents the posh they needed and even allowed their kids to catch and release catfish. I watched as two adventurous boys glided across the water in a canoe. I looked at the dashboard clock. Not in school. Most likely homeschooled kids working on a merit badge of some sort.

My son still loved to fish, and he'd often surprise me with a baggie full of filets from Cedar Lake to fry. He knew I wouldn't clean and gut fish. His father had tried to teach me, but it was a skill I refused to learn.

I parked behind the detached garage, leaving plenty of room for Donetta's maroon SUV or her black MINI Cooper to back out. Her car depended on her mood.

"Where have you been, Belle?" Her shrill voice accosted me when I opened the door. "I'm frantic. I called Ginnie to see if Sukey had finished Prada's grooming and heard about Schotzie. I'll be late to junior league, but I'm going to pick my dog up. I can't lose my baby."

Dropping my purse on the counter, I gave a reassuring smile despite a panicked surge in my stomach. Donetta raving at league could be disastrous. "She's fine. Prettiest poodle there. Her toenails were pink."

Donetta ignored my remarks. "I still can't gamble on her safety. I put the list on the refrigerator." Donetta pulled car keys from her Coach handbag and patted her hair. A whiff of Alexander McQueen perfume met my nose. "I really need those bathrooms to sparkle, honey." She gave me a condescending smile and swept out the door.

I'd learned gritting my teeth gave me a headache, but there were some people who drove you to grit. Donetta was one of those. I'd worked in her home every week for almost a year performing the same tasks, yet she felt compelled to leave a list and expected me to check off what I'd done. Many times I'd purposed to wad up the page, but my heart kept telling me to serve as unto the Lord. Even on marble floors. Now, knowing her temperament and penchant for gossip, I couldn't get my clenched jaw to relax.

I jerked the specially ordered organic cleaning supplies from the laundry room and headed upstairs, my toes sinking in the plush pile carpet. I always worked barefoot from top to bottom in two-story houses. Seemed carefully organized to me.

Organized. As a pastor's wife, I'd found it necessary to be organized. One never knew what duties would befall you on any given day. A hospital visit or a charity dinner—you were always on call, no matter what emergency might be on your list of things to do. Peter's open-door policy had cost me many a night's sleep. I caught myself gritting again.

A good scrubbing of a bathtub relieved much of my tension. I replayed Schotzie's escape as I buffed the mirrors and gold faucets. I slid Donetta's makeup and perfume into the correct drawers. Who could've jimmied the window open? I pictured Donetta scrabbling on a cinder block and laughed.

I stared at my reflection. Pampered Pooch had to be successful. My inheritance depended on the kennel's income for taxes. Those nine acres were all that was left of our family farm. I could hear my brothers scolding me for not selling out when I had the chance. But I wanted that property, my last link to my family. And I couldn't come up with several thousand dollars at a whack. My budget was stretched tighter than a rubber band now.

"We need to find Schotzie." Who could've helped that pooch run for it? Ginnie cared too much about her animals to be careless.

Working my way from bedroom to bedroom, I scoured my brain's junk drawer for details I might've missed. My junk drawer.

In one of my ex-husband's last sermons, he'd mentioned how we needed to search our thoughts and clean out those not pleasing to God. I'd formed a mental picture of an armoire. Unfortunately I'd also pictured a junk drawer where the details of little interest to anyone else resided. From time to time,

I'd pull out one of those thoughts and mull it over to decide if it was a keeper or one to throw out. I'm afraid I seldom threw out any. I'd tried to dust the other areas of my thought life and keep them in line, but the junk drawer spilled forth secrets.

I sighed and surveyed the fresh 460-thread-count linens on the king-size bed. Right now there wasn't one inkling or detail that would lead me to an expensive schnauzer.

Finished with the Robins's home, I drove to the corner store and grabbed a diet soda and a magazine. Hollywood news could ease the tension from my life.

At the house, I propped up on my favorite chair, sipped, and thumbed pages. I'd barely gotten halfway through a story of a young starlet's escapades when the telephone jangled.

Before I could say hello, I heard, "Belle, I'm so worried." Ginnie sniffled loudly on the other end. "Sheriff Connors was still taking my statement when Donetta ripped Prada out of here. She gave me an earful about lack of security for her darling. She'll spread the word—you can bet on that. And of course, there's no sign of Schotzie. What am I going to tell little Linda?"

I slid a store receipt inside the magazine to keep my place and sat forward in my chair. "You just tell them the truth, Ginnie. Someone stole their dog." I chewed on my lower lip, searching my mind for clues. "I am just so surprised there wasn't a barking ruckus when Schotzie got out. Enough to wake you."

"I know, but my bedroom's on the other side of the house. I've gone over it and over it, and I still don't understand how she disappeared right from under my nose." Ginnie hiccupped. "This will ruin my business. I guess it was stupid of me to try to run this place on my own."

My eyelids suddenly heavy, I pulled a blue chenille throw over my legs and settled back. "Ginnie, don't start that second-guessing. This was your idea, your dream to have a kennel." She was a dog lover extraordinaire. Her home had always had more dogs and kids than any other on the block. And now she was making a living from the Fidos of the area. "Since Mitch died and left you the insurance money, it's worked out so far. You've done a bang-up job." I felt my preacher's wife voice kick in. "I know things look bleak at the moment, but there has to be an answer. We'll find it in time."

Ginnie grumbled. "I wish I could be so sure. And I wish it could be before tomorrow when the Lesters drive up." She paused. "My quarterly payment to you looms on the horizon, too. This couldn't have happened at a worse time. Can't God hurry?"

"Don't we all wish God moved in our own time and not His?"

"Peter always said. . ." She paused.

My stomach tightened. "It's okay, sweetie; you can mention his name. I'm not going to hang up." I switched the receiver to my other ear and swallowed hard. "What did Peter always say?"

A small sob escaped. "We serve a nick-of-time God."

I smiled, remembering his earnest face imploring the congregation to believe in an almighty God who would never let them down, who worked in His own timing. A tug at my own heart let me know I'd lost credence in that statement.

"I'm sure Peter was right," I said. "This will all turn out okay, Ginnie. You can file the insurance on the dog and let Linda put it in her bank account for college." *And maybe pay me.*

"But she loved Schotzie so much." A wail set up from the other end of the phone.

"Try to calm down," I said, even knowing my words were useless. "I'll come over tomorrow and be with you when you talk to them, okay?" The idea of having to face Violet made me wince.

"Oh, yes, Belle, please do. I just dread telling Violet's sweet child that her puppy is gone." Ginnie blew her nose once again and strangled out a few more words. "Thank you. You're a real friend."

"Hey, that's what I'm here for. Get some sleep. I'll see you in the morning." As I hung up, I ran a hand through my hair and thought of how many nights Ginnie had been there for me after Peter left. A lump grew in my throat, for my loneliness and her worry. I was so glad we had each other.

Yes, that's what friends are for. I tossed the covers from my legs and headed for the empty bedroom.

I carried a box of fresh pastries to Ginnie's the next day. Dieting could wait until this crisis was over. Ginnie nibbled on a bear claw and kept a wary glance between the clock and the window. About eleven, just before check-out time, a car crunched up the driveway.

Ginnie popped out of her seat to look then threw a glance at me, her eyes wide. "Violet and Linda." She smoothed her hair and trudged to the door before they could knock. I dusted my hands on a napkin and joined her.

Linda bounced in the back door. "Hi, Mrs. Reynolds. Is Schotzie ready?" Her blue-green eyes, outlined in heavy black mascara, sparkled. At her age, I hadn't even owned makeup. Low slung blue jeans and a crop top showed off a belly button. I didn't notice a ring or a tattoo, though.

"Hey, Ginnie. Sorry we're late, but the children were having such fun at their grandmother's. I hated to leave. We don't get over there often enough, but it's a long trip to Little Rock."

Violet followed her daughter inside. "Hello, Belle. Nice to see you." She grinned and focused on Ginnie as she pulled out a checkbook. "How much do I owe you for keeping the beast?"

Ginnie paled and cast a glance at me. I shook my head. Blue eyes implored me. I twisted my lips, and she smiled.

"Well, Linda, Violet, there's been a problem. . ." I began.

"Was Schotzie sick again?" Linda shot an anxious look at her mom. "I told you we should've taken her to Granny's. She mopes and gets sick when she's away from me." She flounced toward Ginnie. "Did you call the vet?"

"Actually, I called the sheriff." Ginnie sank into a kitchen chair and motioned for Violet to sit down.

I placed a hand on the teenager's arm. "Linda, Schotzie's. . .missing."

"What?" The girl swung her arm upward, flinging my hand away. "Missing?" Red-faced, she shrieked at Ginnie, "You lost my dog?"

Ginnie and I exchanged glances.

Linda burst into tears.

"How could that happen? Did you let loose of her leash?" Violet flew to her feet. "Ginnie, explain to me how you lost our dog." She grasped her wailing daughter's elbow. "She's part of our family; we adore her." She sighed and mumbled, "Not to mention how much she's worth."

"Schotzie was *stolen*. Ginnie did not *lose* her," I said in my friend's defense. "Sit down, ladies. We have a lot to discuss." I pulled out two chairs from the dinette. Violet perched on the edge of one, but Linda paced. Ginnie filled them in on the details.

Linda shook with sobs. "How can my baby just disappear?" She stopped and glared at Ginnie. "Did you look *everywhere*?"

Ginnie, slumping further down in her chair, nodded. "Linda, we've searched all over. Even the deputy helped. Sheriff Connors has been out to investigate." I placed a hand on her shoulder. "But we'll keep praying we find her."

Linda flashed me a glance. If looks could kill, I'd be dead.

"You've searched all over?" Violet said, her face

crimson and her fist planted on her hip. "If you'd taken adequate precautions, Schotzie wouldn't have been stolen in the first place." She slung her arm around her daughter's shoulder. "I'll tell you one thing—you can expect to hear from my lawyer."

When the hysterical teen and her distressed mother left, Ginnie began to cry. "I know it's my fault. They have every right to blame me."

"No, it's a thief's fault. You did all you could to protect your property. So stop blaming yourself." I handed her another napkin and tried to console my friend until she calmed down. Under the circumstances, I could see no quick cure to locate Schotzie. And in my mood, I felt my prayers would bounce from the ceiling.

I drove home discouraged. Ginnie and I had tramped the halls of the kennel and the grounds once more. We'd scrutinized the door's latch, scanned the scratch marks, and played detective until we both were frustrated. It seemed Schotzie had disappeared into thin air.

I tossed my purse on a chair and checked my cell phone. Caller ID displayed my son's number, but I decided to check in with him later. First I wanted a long soak in a hot bath.

The first few months of my new business, Belle's Feather Duster, had left me with sore shoulders and an aching back. I'd relied on the bathtub to soothe my muscles. Now I needed it to soothe my mind. I poured bath crystals into the steaming water and tossed a plush yellow towel over the laundry hamper. Sliding out of my tennis shoes and clothes, fatigue grabbed me. I stepped into the hot water.

Somewhere we're missing a detail. If there was anything my sheriff father taught me, it was to notice the details. I slid further down into the steaming tub and reached for my magazine with one dry hand. I chewed my lower lip and stared into space. But which detail?

3

The next morning, Theresa Clarence's freckled face lit up when I appeared at her door. "Hallelujah, help has arrived. Come in, Belle." She pushed back the screen door and waved one hand. "I am afraid the house is extra awful today. Jared and John had a group over, and the results are pretty bad."

I rounded the corner to the kitchen and gazed at the pile of dishes in the sink. "I'll say. What did you do, feed an army?"

Theresa laughed. "Just the youth group. Probably twelve or thirteen." She sighed. "Seems like my kids travel in packs."

"The safest way, if you ask me. Seth was the same."

"Well, we do prefer they be involved with the church group in hopes they'll stay out of trouble." She slid on yellow sandals that matched her capri pants. "But in spite of it, Jared's been distant and moody lately. Locked in his bedroom too much of the time. Jack and I monitor TV and video games, but there's so much to keep track of when you have teenagers. And only two of us." She flung out one hand. "We're outnumbered."

"I remember." Seth had been such a good teenager, but still he'd been pulled to the front door one night by a police officer. He and his best friend had been caught toilet papering a house. While it wasn't against the law in Jackson, it wasn't the best way for a preacher's kid to spend his free time. Peter had been furious.

Theresa bagged pizza boxes. "I think I'd better pick up some paper plates for next time we host the group." She poked trash into a black plastic bag. "Jared said he'd ask Charlie Baker to come to the youth party. He works for Ginnie, doesn't he?"

I nodded, loathe to discuss Pampered Pooch.

"Seems like a hardworking kid." She slung the trash bag into the garage.

I smiled. "Trying to take my job?" I rolled up the sleeves of my denim shirt and ran soapy water in the sink to soak the sticky plates. "Don't worry about this. You go visit your mother. How's she doing?"

"The same. Old age isn't for sissies, but she isn't letting it get her down." She lifted a bag from the stove top. "I'm taking her leftover chocolate chip cookies I hid from the kids. She'll be the most popular senior citizen at the center this afternoon." Purse on her shoulder, she scoured for her keys. "See you later." She started for the door and then stopped. "And your bag of cookies is hidden in the empty flour canister." She winked and left.

I smiled. What a difference in clientele. Theresa was always so thoughtful. I found a cookie, popped it in my mouth, and then faced the duties ahead of me. I'd save the pile in the kitchen for last. Heading down the long hall to the bedrooms, I waited for the dogs to greet me. No barks or whines from two loping dalmatians. I wondered how Schotzie fared. Was she in wide-open spaces or locked in someone's den?

I opened the boys' bedroom door and surveyed the

mound of dirty clothes on the floor and the twin beds. It looked as if a wrestling match had taken place and the linens had lost. I pulled off the sheets, gathered the clothes, and carried them to the laundry room. While I did not wash clothes, I did take them where they belonged. Evidently the Clarence boys didn't understand the hamper concept.

Humming a hymn, I made short work of the three bedrooms. Cleaning relaxed me. There was something about restoring order to a house that gave me a real sense of accomplishment. I'd never been a neat freak, but I'd always kept a tidy home that made Peter proud. *At least he complimented me for that.*

And I was proud I'd used my skill to begin a business. Not that I'd had a lot of choices once he left. What else was I trained to do? I jerked the last comforter over the master bedroom's bed. I had dusted off my pride, printed some business cards, and given them out.

I stood, one hand rubbing the small of my back. Talk about swallowing my pride. I cringed as I recalled meeting one of the women from our congregation in the grocery store. I'd handed her a card with a flourish.

She read it and then drilled me with a stare. "Cleaning houses?" She looked down her nose. "I suppose you do have to make money. But a pastor's wife shouldn't clean toilets for a living. Aren't you capable in some other area?"

Capable? I wanted to scream at the woman. *Yes, I was a capable wife.* Instead I smiled, retrieved my card from her hand, and walked away worried I'd bite a hole in my tongue.

Now my full schedule left little room for self-pity and fueled my bank account, though it was not premium grade fuel. And it certainly wouldn't cover taxes on nine acres.

A tangle of emotions swept over me as I waltzed down memory lane. I scrubbed the bathroom mirror vigorously. When my arm tired, I groaned and stuck my tongue out at my damp reflection. "How are you going to find a dog thief?"

The back door slammed, and I heard a clatter of keys hit the kitchen counter.

"Belle?" Theresa called.

"Back here. In your bathroom." I gave a last swipe to the mirror and went to meet her.

"Are the dogs in here with you?" She met me in the hallway.

"No, I haven't seen them all morning. I figured they were outside."

Theresa's brown eyes widened. "They aren't in the dog run. I went back there to put dog food in the storage unit. I know Jared put them there before he left for school. He knew you were coming." She wheeled about and headed to the patio door. I followed with a sinking premonition in my stomach.

Flower beds bordered the manicured backyard. A small white gazebo sat in the middle. Sweet fragrances came from the variety of flowers dancing in the breeze. The chain-link dog runs took up fifteen or twenty feet of the side yard. The Clarences had been breeding dalmatians, and they needed plenty of exercise room for the two dogs. Both runs were empty, gates shut.

"What in the world?" Theresa shot a frantic glance at me.

My mind flickered to Schotzie, and the knot in my stomach tightened. Could it be possible two more dogs had vanished?

Indeed it was possible. After the boys came home, they mounted an extensive search of the neighborhood. No spotted friends rushed to meet them. I told Theresa about Schotzie, and she phoned the sheriff's office. Don soon stood on the front porch.

"Belle, you stealing dogs to supplement your income?" He grinned and took off his cap as he entered the living room.

I shook my head. "Not funny, Don." I looked at the boys sitting on the sofa. "They're pretty upset."

Theresa said, "We have no idea what's happened to our dogs, Deputy, but in light of Ginnie's story, I thought we'd better report this. Not only do we love them like family, but they are worth a great deal of money." Her fingers beat a rhythm on the arm of her chair. "I dread telling my husband when he gets home." Her voice was flat. John glanced up with a stricken look. Jared's face went rigid.

"Well, show me where they were, and let's walk through the scene." He turned toward me. "Seems like we've done this bit before."

I trailed behind the family and Don to the dog runs, watching Jared. Don flipped the latches, and Jared blew a bubble. Pink. I nudged Don's elbow and lifted an eyebrow. He glanced at the boy, raised a brow, then turned back to the fencing.

"Sturdy. Can't be nosed up by a dog." He made a note on his pad. "Were there locks?"

Theresa shook her head. "Our gate to the yard has a lock, but we don't keep them on the runs." She sighed. "Guess we should've, but I never considered anyone in Trennan stealing them."

"We've got crime here, too." Don's chest puffed out a tad, his badge glistening in the sun. "Growing city brings in trouble, and we have to stay on top of it."

I stepped to the gate. The lock was unhitched. I looked at the boys. "This gate's open. Was it this way before you left for school?"

John wiped his hands on his jeans and shook his head. "I don't know. Jared put them out today."

"Not my fault. You had the four-wheeler yesterday. You used the gate last," Jared sniped back.

Theresa glared at her sons, arms folded across her chest. "You mean you don't know if the gate was locked or not?"

Chagrined, the boys shook their heads.

"Go inside." Her jaw tightened. "We'll talk when Dad gets here." She ran a hand through her hair and pinched the bridge of her nose. Once the boys were gone, she muttered, "Teenagers. They're never responsible for anything that happens."

Don snorted. "Seems like normal to me. Not

many of them are."

I put one arm around Theresa's shoulders, again the consoling preacher's wife. "I'm so sorry. Maybe you can channel that energy creatively. Let them make some posters to hang up and advertise the dogs as missing."

"Great idea." She wiped away a tear. "I think I'll go talk to them now." She stepped toward the house and paused. "Thank you, Belle, for always saying the right thing."

I nodded and smiled.

Don walked the length of the dog run and back to me. "Good idea about the posters, Belle, and good catch on the bubblegum." He jotted another few words. "Maybe Ginnie needs to get posters up, too. I'm going to take this report back to the office." He shut his notebook and slid the pen into his shirt pocket. "I have more work to do and can't get all het up over missing dogs."

A flash of irritation flickered in my head. "Don, you have to understand—these aren't just your everyday mutts from the pound." I tapped his notebook. "The combined value of these two dogs and Schotzie exceeds your monthly paycheck."

He blew a low whistle and hitched his belt. "Guess I'd better bring out my bloodhound then." He chuckled. "Don't worry, Belle, I'm going to question our bubblegum bandit—see where he was last night."

I sighed, "Right here eating pizza probably."

Don ambled toward the gate. "I'll be back to see what he has to say."

Shaking my head, I walked inside and found John

and his mother bent over the kitchen table with poster board and markers. "Any way I can help?"

Theresa slid my paycheck to me. "I'll double this if you stay and deal with Jared's attitude." She hastily brushed a tear from her cheek. "You've been a great help already. Thanks for being here." She completed the phone number on the poster. "If you'll take this one sign and hang it on the corner when you go, I'd appreciate it."

"Glad to." I picked up the poster and a pushpin. "I hope the dogs turn up soon." Neither answered.

I stopped my car at the corner and tugged the poster board from the backseat. As I tacked it to the telephone pole next to the signpost of Cedar and Crosswell, a heaviness shrouded me. I stepped back and surveyed the crooked letters. Who would take a pet from a child?

Guess meanness has invaded Trennan, too.

4

My Jeep shuddered to a stop in the driveway, and I groaned, a nervous shiver tickling my stomach. With nearly 150,000 miles on the odometer, I had to baby her, and I didn't have time or money for car repairs. Maybe I'd ask my neighbor, Mel, to test drive it. He'd tinkered with it before and had her purring. When I discovered my brother's high school buddy living next door, I had no idea how invaluable a friend he'd become to me. I glanced toward his house and saw his truck wasn't in the driveway. I'd have to wait till evening.

My purse caught on the steering wheel, and I turned to pull it loose. Fiddling with the strap, I settled back against the seat and viewed my house. It needed painting. Another nerve prickled. More expense. I batted my eyelashes against tears.

I'd chosen the plantation-style house because I loved the front porch and pillars and because it was so different from my previous home. The wide windows invited in the morning sunshine. Two black wrought-iron rockers sat at one end of the wide porch, a low table in between. They'd been used often before. Peter and I had whiled away many a pleasant evening in those when we lived by the church, visitors dropping by unannounced. Not anymore. I didn't regret my twenty-five-mile move from Jackson to Trennan. No, after Peter's departure, I wanted to be lost in a sea of new faces and find a different church home. I'd settled in nicely here. Although not all my neighbors were new. I wrinkled my nose as I thought of my in-laws. They'd chosen to move out of Jackson, too. Our paths seldom crossed, and for that I was glad.

I heaved a sigh and walked toward the house, the sad face of John Clarence and surly attitude of Jared mingling with heaviness from my heart. Circulars and a few envelopes peeked from the mailbox by the front door. I retrieved them and tucked them under my arm. Unlocking the back door, I cast a look at the paint peeling from the door frame and frowned.

I tossed the pile on the kitchen counter and ruffled through the envelopes. Junk mail. So many wasted trees to tell me of low-interest credit card rates and superlow car insurance. I swept the pile into the garbage can, grabbed a glass, poured a diet cola, and added ice cubes.

I sat at the table and pulled a pile of bills in front of me. Real mail. Things I needed to deal with and didn't want to face. Money, as usual, was tight. I didn't lack for anything, but I never had extra. And now taxes on the property to worry about?

"God provides, Belle. We'll make it through." Peter's voice echoed in my brain with his oft-used phrase. He was right, of course. God had provided so much for Seth and me when I'd become single again. I cringed at the phrase. Single again. As if there'd been a choice once Miranda appeared.

I shoved the bill pile toward the salt and pepper shakers. I'd deal with the cold hard facts tomorrow, like a true Scarlett O'Hara.

As I headed to the den, I passed the phone and remembered Seth's call, which I hadn't returned. He might find the theft of the dogs interesting. The *Jackson News* was always looking for a scoop. And bubblegum on security cameras was a real twist.

Drink in hand, I stretched out on the blue-and-white checked sofa and dialed his office.

"Good afternoon, *Jackson News*." Pepper's singsong greeting made me smile. I pictured the tiny, dark-haired girl swallowed by a desk chair, swinging her legs. Her name belied her intelligence. She was a top-notch reporter.

"Pepper, this is Mrs. Blevins. Is Seth available?"

A giggle escaped her lips. "He's in his office pounding on the keyboard, but I know he'll take your call. Just one second." A moment of music sounded in my ear.

"Mom," my son's deep voice boomed. "What's up?"

"Hey, kiddo, sorry I didn't call back last night. I was pooped." I sipped my drink, kicked off my tennis shoes, and wiggled my toes. "Anything you needed?"

"Just checking in."

I heard the squeak of his chair and pictured him reared back, one hand behind his head. His habits mirrored his father's, as did his appearance. Tall and broad-shouldered, my blond-haired, blue-eyed boy had developed into a very handsome man.

"Seth, the strangest thing happened at Ginnie's kennel." I relayed Schotzie's story.

"Oh man, I know Ginnie and her dogs. I bet this

is eating her up." Seth's voice hardened. "I'll need to get information from Sheriff Connors. Tampering with security cameras." He puffed out a breath.

"Ginnie's over the top. And stranger still, today the Clarences' dalmatians turned up missing."

The chair groaned. "Mother, we've had reports of three dogs taken here in Jackson." He paused, and I heard the tapping of computer keys. "Yeah, one standard poodle, one American Eskimo, and. . ."

"An Eskimo dog in Jackson?" Cold-weather breeds didn't seem to fit in our neck of the woods.

"And a Newfoundland. All missing in the last week and a half." Seth blew out a sigh. "Those are pricey animals, too."

"Newfoundlands and Eskimo dogs? How in the world do they handle Tennessee heat? I thought they'd need cooler climates. But what do I know about dogs?" I swirled the cola and ice in my glass and took a swallow. Just the thought of all that dog hair made me hot.

"Breeds of all kinds are raised around here. When I had the local interest beat, I reported on many a dog show, remember?" He chuckled. "Stepped in poop and got nipped on the ankle from that beastly Chihuahua but got a date with its owner."

"I'd forgotten about that." I smiled. Lauren Cooper had been a nice young lady. Her family had farmed up the road from my uncle for years. "What ever happened to Lauren?" What a cutie pie she'd been. Curly hair, freckled nose.

"I believe she has a husband and a kid now."

I sighed.

"Mother, don't start pining." Seth's voice dropped a notch. "Lauren wasn't the right woman for me."

"Well I don't know what you're looking for in a girl, but she seemed like a pretty good fit to me." *Seth and Lauren's babies would've been so precious.*

"I'll know the right one when I meet her, so please, just drop it." Seth paused, and I could hear the clicking keyboard again. "Hang on while I get your side of Ginnie's story. I'll want to interview her for the article."

I waited then ran through the facts and rattled off Ginnie's phone number and tagged on Theresa's information.

After the last question, he said, "All these dogs disappearing. If they were just mutts, it would be one thing, but man, the cost of some of these animals." He snorted. "You can pay over a thousand dollars for one."

"So I've heard. Ginnie told me Schotzie was really expensive. I can't even imagine spending that much money on a dog." I shrugged and sipped my drink. Imagine what I could do with that much money. Pay taxes? "We loved Patches when you were little, but he came from the pound." I smiled remembering a towheaded boy and his black-and-white dog trudging down the gravel road at his grandpa's. A prick of sorrow nipped my heart. That very gravel road was in jeopardy.

"Dog breeding can be big business."

I shifted on the sofa. "The whole dog business is astounding. Ginnie's day camp has customers. She's even considering webcams so owners can see their pets while they're away."

"Webcams? Seriously? I saw the brochure about

the Pampered Pooch; maybe I need to visit." I heard a smile in his voice. "Ginnie deserves to make good money from that venture." He paused. "You know, I could consider a feature article about her unusual business. We haven't covered it yet."

"Oh, Seth, Ginnie'd be excited about the publicity. But maybe we'd better wait until the Schotzie mess is straightened out." I didn't want him probing too far and worrying about my loss of revenue. He wasn't fully informed of my business dealings since I'd not heeded his caution about leasing land to Ginnie.

"True. I think I'm going to call Kevin to see if he's heard anything about the dog thefts in Trennan." A drawer clunked. "I have his number somewhere in here." A rustle of papers. "If I get him, do you want to meet us for lunch this week?"

"No, thanks." I hadn't seen my tall detective nephew in a while. Not since he'd moved up the ranks in the Jackson police department.

"Just Kevin, Mom, not Aunt Phoebe."

I raised the cold glass to my forehead and rolled it back and forth. The chill reminded me of my ex-sister-in-law. She could freeze a person with her pointed looks. And she'd frosted me one time too many.

"No, Seth. I don't want to have lunch." I tried to sound chipper. "But I appreciate the invitation. Why don't you come by later this week for dinner?"

"Belle Blevins, you know the way to your child's heart." Seth laughed. "Sure, I'd love to have dinner with you. But why don't we go out? I know you've been putting in long hours, and let's face it, cooking isn't on your top ten list of favorite things to do."

He'd pegged me there. I hated being in the kitchen. I knew how to hold a spatula and when to slice and dice, but I didn't enjoy the chore anymore.

"Okay, honey. I appreciate your thoughtfulness." I placed my glass on the end table. "Call me and let me know when and where I can meet you."

A silence hung in the air. "You sure you don't want to see Kevin? You could give him the Trennan scoop yourself. Might be nice to get together."

I frowned. "Stop mending fences, Seth. One of these days I'll be ready. But not today."

"I understand. Love you, Mom."

The dial tone echoed in my ear for a few seconds before I realized he was gone. I'd been woolgathering. *No, some fences were better left broken.* Peter's family had laid too much blame on me when he left. The hurt ran deep.

I shoved off the couch and set my empty glass in the sink. The sound of a lawn mower rumbled through the back door. Mel was cutting his grass. I think he loved his riding lawn mower almost as much as he did his satellite TV. The minute a blade of grass poked its head up high enough, Mel fired up his machine. I could still picture him astride a horse in the rodeo arena. He'd team roped with my brother, Marcus, and they'd almost won the state championship their senior year. Mel had eaten many a meal at our house—even some I'd cooked.

Sliding into my tennis shoes, I stepped outside to see if we could arrange a time for him to check out my car. I waited alongside the driveway while he finished cutting a swath down one side of his yard. He glanced my way, and I waved. The lawn mower puttered to a stop.

"Hey, Belle, you need something?"

I pointed to the Jeep. "*She* needs something, but I don't know what. Do you have any time to check her out?"

He grinned. "Sure, let me finish here, and I'll come get the keys."

"Thank you."

He nodded, started the mower, and continued his route.

The smell of gasoline wafted through the air but was soon covered by the sweet smell of cut grass, which tickled my nose. Spring evenings, daylight savings time, fireflies circling, laughter from Mel's girls as they raced on skates down the drive. A wave of melancholy engulfed my heart. I missed having a family.

Mel's wife appeared on the front lawn. She flagged him down and called, "Dinner's ready." The mower ground to a halt, and Mel's face darkened.

"Don't worry about the car, Mel." I waved at him. I surely didn't want him fiddling under the hood in his present mood.

"Will check on it later, Belle. Be sure of it." He stomped his feet on the porch, grass and muck flying, then disappeared inside.

I pulled a garden hose from beneath the boxwood hedge and began to water the flower beds. The petunias perked up. They certainly didn't rival Theresa Clarence's, but they added color to my yard. I made water loops,

spelling out *Seth* then *Lauren* and finally *dogs*. I skipped
Peter.

———

Before I crawled into bed, I called Ginnie. Since
Mitch's death, we often closed our evenings with a
check-in chat.

"Any news of Schotzie?"

A deep sigh came through the receiver. "Nope.
Nothing yet. And Violet's called and given me the riot
act. As if I'd planned this." Discouragement tainted her
words.

"I worked the Clarence's house today, and their
dalmatians are missing."

She gasped.

"I wanted to fill in Seth with the latest, so I called
to tell him. Well, seems there's been a rash of missing
dogs over his way, too." I tugged the pale yellow comforter from my bed and folded it over the quilt rack.
"He planned to ask Kevin to go to lunch, see if he
knows anything." I bit my lip and added, "Seth wants
more details from you after he talks to the sheriff."

"Oh no. I didn't think about news coverage." She
sniffled. "More negative news. All I need."

"Once this is cleared up, Seth said he'd run a
feature article about Pampered Pooch. That'll be good
publicity."

"*If* it's cleared up. I've heard of people stealing dogs.
They call it dognapping. Is that what they think?"

I slid into bed. "Sure does sound like it. Or it's a

mighty huge coincidence, which I don't believe."

"Oh, Belle, then there's less likelihood of recovering Schotzie. I think I feel sick." Ginnie's moan pulled at my heart.

"Honey, I didn't call to make you sick; I just wanted to keep you up-to-date." I plumped two pillows behind me and sat up. "If the police department in Jackson gets involved, they can help Don and the sheriff."

"What would you do with AKC dogs? Reckon they sell them for pets?"

"No clue. But I might ask some people." I closed my eyes and ran through the Rolodex of pet lovers I knew.

"Belle?" Ginnie spoke softly. "Would you pray?"

I smiled, warmth spreading through me. "Yes, honey. I'd be glad to." We ended our evening asking God for wisdom and protection and closed with praises. "Think you'll sleep?"

"You bet. I'll call you tomorrow. Good night."

Placing the phone in its cradle, I snuggled down and reached for the lamp. *Lord, please help Ginnie find that dog. I know all creatures great and small are Your concern. Protect Schotzie. We need to get her back. I need to get her back.*

Now I was praying pet prayers along with money prayers.

5

I awoke, a dagger stabbing my left eye. With my thumb, I pressed my eye socket. I recognized the symptoms.

Great, a migraine.

I seldom had the painful things, but when I did, I got rid of them with a prescription painkiller. I stumbled to the bathroom to locate the medicine. Pressing the pill from the foil-covered container with one eye closed was a feat. The manufacturers must not understand that when your head is falling off your shoulders, you don't need the extra aggravation of childproof packaging. I managed to pop one in my mouth and scooped water from the faucet. Fumbling my way back to the bedroom, I stretched across the bed to wait for the medicine to kick in.

Today was my twenty-seventh wedding anniversary. Small wonder I'd awakened in pain. A lone tear slid down my temple. I flung one arm over my eyes, choking back a sob. The aggravation and worry about money welled up. I needed that dog to be found so Pampered Pooch's reputation wouldn't be marred. I massaged my left temple as my thoughts wandered. The cinder blocks under the window had given a boost to the thieves, so they didn't have to be as tall as Don. But to climb inside the narrow opening, they'd have to be agile. Then pull the dog out. And do what with her?

I tugged a pillow closer and drew in deep breaths,

Lamaze style. *Relax. Turn off the brain. Let the pain drift away. Forget the anniversary date; it doesn't matter anymore. Breathe.* Thoughts skittered through my mind—dogs, taxes, Peter, his new bride. *Breathe.*

That lasted ten minutes. Dragging on white jeans and a red T-shirt, I shoved my feet into tennis shoes and bit back the remaining pain. Someone I knew would shed light on a market for missing dogs.

Chirping parakeets greeted me inside Weston's store along with the smell of cat litter. I wrinkled my nose. Ebony, Harley's huge black cat, wound her way down the aisle, queen of the store.

I threaded my way toward the back around bags of dog food and cages with hamsters and gerbils. *Eww, rodents.* A chill raced up my arms. I sidestepped to another aisle.

"Hey, Belle. What brings you in? Ready for a puppy?" Harley's booming voice carried above the cacophony of sounds.

I smiled, remembering the pet prayers, and then waltzed with Ebony toward the register, she weaving in and out of my steps. "No, Harley, not yet. I don't want anything I need to feed or water." I looked down. Black cat hair clung to my white pant legs.

"Shucks, I just knew I could bring you over to the pet side this time." He grinned a lopsided grin. I'd known Harley since high school. Big and brawny, he'd played defensive end on our football team. Now muscle had turned to fat, his chest giving way to gravity and drooping to waist level. I'd seldom seen him without a plaid shirt and a smile.

"Now, Harley, I love animals. Had plenty on the farm, and we even had pets when Seth was little. I just don't want any extra responsibilities right now. Cleaning up after other people makes me want to keep my life simple." I scooped up the cat and stroked her back. "See? Ebony knows I'm an animal lover." The cat jumped from my arms and dashed away, circling back around behind the counter.

Harley laughed. "She knows, all right."

I smothered the urge to stick out my tongue at Ebony and changed the subject. "Do you know about the missing dogs in town? The Clarence boys' dalmatians are gone."

A frown crossed his face. "Yeah, I heard. Don gave me a call last night." Harley swiped at the counter with a towel. "I feel bad for those kids. Their dad is pretty hard on them. He'll be ticked over this."

I gnawed my lower lip. "Maybe Theresa will soften the blow."

He pointed at a bulletin board. "Mrs. Clarence is bringing me a poster. Don told me about Ginnie's deal, too," Harley said. "Hate to hear a dog was stolen from the kennel. That'll be bad for her business."

I nodded. "She's plenty worried." I stepped closer. "Why would anyone steal dogs?" I held out one hand.

His frown deepened. "Research labs want them."

"What?" I shuddered at the thoughts my mind conjured up.

Harley snapped his fingers, and Ebony jumped on

the counter. He rubbed her ears. "Yeah, people can sell animals for research, sad to say. But the Clarence dogs are purebred, so they might go to the black market."

"What black market?"

Harley crossed his arms, a scowl flickering on his face. "In the new world of computers, there are ways to falsify documents." He pointed at me. "The Internet has made crooks real happy—know what I mean? Low-down scum." He shook his head. "You get a good dog with great conformation, make up a pedigree, and—boom—you're on your way to the flea market getting high dollars. Belle, there's big money in showing dogs. I mean big money." Harley pursed his lips. "Those dog shows in Memphis, why, they bring in dogs from all over. People spend thousands of dollars not only buying the dog but getting it certified."

"What's certified?"

"They earn so many points at a dog show and get certified with the AKC. And they've got to have points to get to be a champion. After that, their value skyrockets." He snapped his fingers, and Ebony meowed. We both laughed.

"So skyrocketing value means. . . ?" I tipped my head and shrugged.

"Then you can breed 'em or use them for breeding. The stud fees can be huge." Harley pulled a toothpick from his shirt pocket and stuck it in his mouth, rolling it back and forth. "And that dog of Violet's, well, her puppies would go for seven, eight hundred each. Might have three or four pups, maybe more."

"I had no idea. This is a whole new world." Poor

Schotzie, mother of many. No wonder Violet nearly had a seizure.

"It is a whole world." He chuckled, the toothpick lolling on his lips. "And an expensive one. The dog handlers, the ones who show the dogs in the ring, waltz away with a pretty penny, too. A gal I know over near Atlanta shows those Jack Russell dogs." He spread his hands a few inches apart. "Little ole dogs. Anyway, the owner of one bought a fully-loaded RV for her to use to travel to shows." He pulled the toothpick out and waved it in the air. "She got paid and was shuttled around the country free."

I gave a low whistle. "Sounds like an interesting way to make a living."

"If you like travel and dogs. You go to one of those shows and you'll see acres of RVs." Harley glanced around the shop. "Me, I want to be home too much." He shoved away from the counter. "Why you so interested in these dogs, Belle?"

"I don't know." I sighed and fingered a dog tag on display. "I want Pampered Pooch to succeed." Little did he know how much. "And Seth said dogs were missing in Jackson and then here in Trennan, too. Guess I was just curious as to why." I didn't meet his eye.

"Don't you be asking *why* too much, Belle Blevins." He shook a finger at me. "I've known you to get too all-fired curious. Don't go looking for trouble."

I swatted at Harley's hand. "Me? Trouble? Not a chance." I swung my purse off my shoulder and turned to leave. "Thanks for the information, Harley. Bye, Ebony." The cat turned tail and sashayed away.

6

My arms filled with grocery sacks, I juggled the key to the front door.

"Need help, Belle?" Mel hollered.

I propped the sacks on my knee and looked his way. "Think I've got it, but thanks."

"I have time to look at the Jeep if you're ready." He headed across the yard. "Unlock the door, then toss me the keys."

I examined his face for signs of a foul mood. "You sure?" I jiggled the knob.

"I'm sure. I just finished the last of the trimming." He turned toward his house. "Looks pretty fair, don't you think?"

I knew how proud Mel was of his landscaping, so I pretended to survey the grounds. "I think it's mighty fine, Mel. You do such a good job. Don't know how you manage it."

He dropped his gaze and shoved his hands in the pockets of his shorts. "Aw, it ain't much. I like being outside. It's a good thing, too, since Belinda loves a nice yard." He walked to my car. "Now get me the keys."

I toed the door open, letting one sack slide to the kitchen floor. I pivoted and threw the keys in Mel's direction. To my amazement, he caught them midair. "Good catch." I smiled.

"Thanks. I practiced." He laughed and opened the Jeep door.

While Mel fiddled with the car, I put away groceries. I didn't have much to buy nowadays, with just me to feed, but the temptation to fill my pantry was a hard one to break. I'd enjoyed feeding my small family even though cooking wasn't my favorite activity. Now I stacked soup cans on the shelves and frozen dinners for one in the freezer.

The phone's shrill ring startled me. I saw Seth's number on the ID screen and grabbed the receiver. "Hey, honey. How's your day going?"

"Pretty fine. How about you?"

His affectionate tone made me smile. My number one kid was my number one love. "Just got in from the store." I slid a tub of butter in the refrigerator and added a carton of diet soda.

Seth's chair creaked. "Why don't we go to lupper after a while?"

I laughed. When we'd been a family, Peter's meetings dictated our mealtime, and sometimes we ate early. If he'd skipped lunch, he'd call it lupper, lunch and supper combined.

I crumbled plastic bags into one another and tossed them onto the floor of the pantry. "I'm game. Where?"

"How about Grady's?"

His favorite family-style restaurant was short on ambience but served great food. "I really like their chicken-fried steak and gravy." I frowned and thought of my jeans going up another size. "So much for any dieting if I choose that place."

"You aren't dieting anyway, are you?"

Thoughts of donuts fluttered through my mind. "Not right now. Especially if we're going to Grady's." I smiled.

"Mom." Seth sighed. "You're a mess. You don't need any diet."

"Thanks for the vote of confidence."

He chuckled. "I could pick you up if you'd like."

I heard the roar of my Jeep as Mel started the engine. "You know, that might be a great idea. Mel's tinkering with the car right now, and he might not be finished. I don't want to rush him, either, and be rude." I glanced out the door and saw that the hood was raised. "If you don't mind coming this way, I'd appreciate a ride."

"Sure thing. I'll pick you up about four thirty. How's that?"

"Sounds great to me. Thanks, sweetie."

When I walked outside, Mel's head was bent over the running motor. I hollered, "Mel?"

He raised his head quickly and almost cracked it on the hood. "You scared me, Belle." He rubbed a greasy hand on the leg of his jeans. "I think this carburetor needs some work. Shouldn't take me too long."

I nodded as though I understood. "Seth's coming to take me out for dinner. Will you need me here for any reason?"

"No, I've got it nailed down. If I need a part, I'll get it and you can pay me later."

I laughed. "As long as it isn't a new motor, we'll be fine."

Mel tapped his fingers on the fender. "Did some

work for your friend, Ginnie, last week."

"I didn't know that."

"Her riding lawn mower wouldn't start. Belinda told her I tinkered with motors last time she had Mustard groomed."

Mustard, the baying beagle who raced through the neighborhood, went in periodically for a wash and dip so she could sleep at the foot of their bed. Mel's expression when he'd confessed their dog slept with them was hilarious.

"She appreciated the help, I'm sure."

"I appreciated the business. Would've appreciated it more had she paid me."

His bitter tone surprised me. "She's been distracted lately. I'm sure she'll take care of your bill."

Mel's eyes darkened. "Ginnie can be mighty snooty when she wants to. I had some dealings with Mitch when he was alive and crossed her path more than once. Always thought then she needed to come off her high horse. Seems like nothing much has changed."

Startled, I could think of no response.

He tugged some small cards from his pocket. "I'm starting a honey-do business since I'm an expert, what with Belinda's lists." He handed them to me, a smudge of oil on the corner of the top one. "Pass these out for me, would ya?" He snorted. "But I'd prefer paying customers."

I read the small print. "You're going to come out of retirement? What about your yard? Why, a blade of grass might crop up and you'd not notice."

His lips twisted in a half smile. "Well, truth be

told, I can use the income." He shot a look toward his house. "My wife loves the new mall over toward Jackson."

Again I had no reply. Belinda's love of fine things was no surprise. I left him alone muttering about oil and belts. *Lord, You know what's in my bank account and what could be needed. Get ole Betsy running without too much expense. And bless Mel for his willing spirit. Bless his new business venture. But what's this animosity against my friend?* Uneasiness rode in my chest. I'd have to ask Ginnie about this strange turn of events.

Before Seth arrived, I freshened up. I swept on fresh makeup and even added some eyeliner and mascara. With my blue linen pantsuit Ginnie had insisted I buy, I felt presentable for a date with my boy. I sat on the sofa, curtain pulled to one side, and watched for his arrival. I could hear tools hit the ground as Mel worked.

My gaze flitted about the room, settling on Seth's college graduation picture. He stood next to me, taller by about six inches, his chin resting on the top of my head. It was one of his favorite positions. He said I had a niche in my skull that made a great head rest. His navy blue eyes were so like his dad's. A well of sadness rose up as I recalled graduation day. Seth had tried to bridge the uncomfortable gap between Peter and me, Miranda standing to one side. To her credit, she didn't horn in on the festivities, but I resented her presence at the important occasion. Seth, polite and thoughtful, thanked her for coming but did not invite them to join his roommates and me for dinner. I'm ashamed to admit it, but I was proud to be the chosen parent. I'm sure I gloated. Did I repent later? I chewed my lower lip.

It was no accident my son was taking me to dinner on this date. He knew the significance of April 30, my anniversary.

I heard him arrive and headed outside. He'd gotten out to talk cars with Mel.

Seth peered into the motor. "You send me a bill if Mom's car needs more than she can handle. I can buy parts." He fingered one of Mel's new business cards.

"Seth!" I blushed. "I can take care of my own bills. I told Mel I'd reimburse him."

Mel laughed. "I might charge you both." He eyed me then said, "You look mighty pretty tonight, Belle. That blue shirt makes your eyes shine. Must be seeing this good-looking kid that put a grin on your face."

I grinned wider. "Mel, you're so sweet. Go tell Belinda how gorgeous she is, too." His wife was beautiful. Her Puerto Rican perpetual tan and jet black hair set her apart from most in Trennan.

"Oh, I tell her that all the time." He waved a greasy rag. "Y'all get going. Seth said Grady's was waiting." He gave a theatric sigh. "Wish I had a chicken-fried steak to look forward to."

"I can bring dinner home for you," I offered.

"Oh no. Belinda would have my head." His mouth drew in a tight line. "She's got me on this low-cholesterol diet. You know, the kind where you eat rabbit food and cardboard. Guess I'd better stick to it and make her happy. No, you just go on and clog those arteries. I'll be fine."

Seth and I laughed and walked to his car.

"He's a real cut up but a great neighbor to you, Mom," Seth said as he opened the door.

I slid in the front seat. "That he is." But his attitude needed as much adjustment as my carburetor evidently did.

We drove toward Jackson, the evening traffic beginning to build. Kudzu covered much of the landscape alongside the road like green frosting sliding up and down tree trunks. I knew the state Department of Transportation had a hard time keeping one step in front of the green monster. It was a joke in our neck of the woods that if you stood still long enough, you'd be kudzu-covered.

Seth broke the silence. "Mom, how was your day?" His soft tone indicated more to the question.

"I did fine, dear." A flood of gratitude for this great kid welled up. "Thanks for asking."

He reached over and squeezed my hand. "I'm glad to hear that." He released my fingers and shifted in his seat. "I invited Kevin to join us."

"Seth." I frowned.

"Not for any reason other than to talk about the missing dogs, Mom. I didn't get a chance to meet with him the other day, and I wanted to see what he knew. He called after you and I talked, so I invited him." His stony face gave no room for argument.

My mind raced, and I decided to keep quiet. "I think that's fine. I have some more information to add anyway."

Seth glanced away from the road at me. "What new information?"

"I'll tell you both at dinner."

"Mother, you are not getting involved in the investigation of missing pooches, are you?" Seth's brow furrowed. "Why, there's no telling what's really going on. You just need to stay out of it and read the stories in the paper."

"Don't tell me what I should do, son," I snapped. "I've had quite enough of that in my lifetime."

A beat of silence, then he said, "Sorry."

I sighed. "I'm sorry, too. That was rude." I toyed with my purse strap. "I just asked a few questions, that's all. I wanted more to tell Ginnie, so I talked to Harley at the pet shop." And I wanted to find out where to look for an expensive schnauzer. "I'll explain what I know when we meet Kevin."

"All right." He swung into the restaurant parking lot. "I just worry about you sometimes, Mom."

"Well, I worry about me most days, son." I laughed. "But so far, the good Lord's brought me through."

He grinned. "Yeah, He has done that."

We stepped from the car and walked into Grady's. The older restaurant resembled a log cabin with a huge dining room. White, paper-covered rectangular tables were scattered around the room. Grady's wasn't a fancy sit-and-be-waited-on place.

The pungent smell of barbecue filled the air. I inhaled and figured I gained two pounds just sniffing. A dry erase board sat on a large easel with the specials of the day scrawled in red. Seth read them, but I already knew my order. I loved their barbecue, but tonight chicken-fried steak called to me. We waited in line until it was time to order. I grabbed my cup of sweet tea and found us a place to sit while Seth gathered our silverware and napkins. The intercom called out a number, and I retrieved our food, my salivary glands working overtime.

As we settled at the table, Kevin's voice carried across the room.

"Aunt Belle, Seth."

I looked up to see my nephew and another gentleman head in our direction. I propped my arms on the table and mustered a smile.

"How are you, Kevin?"

He reached down and gave me a peck on the cheek. "I'm great, Aunt Belle." He motioned to the man standing beside him. "I'd like for you to meet a friend of mine, Franklin Jeffries."

Franklin extended his hand to Seth and then to me. "How do you do?"

I managed a small smile and dipped my head toward my plate. A wave of shyness swallowed me. Being around good-looking strangers was uncomfortable now that the wife cloak no longer draped about me.

Kevin and Franklin lined up at the counter to place their order, and I gave the man a once-over. He was about Seth's height, brown hair feathered with gray, and very fit and tan. When he swung his glance in my direction, I felt his stare and looked away, heat creeping in my cheeks. They gathered their trays and returned to our table.

Seth and Kevin sat beside one another, leaving Franklin to pull out a chair next to me. I slid my napkin into my lap and was surprised when he extended his hand. "Would you join me in grace?" he said.

The boys joined hands with us, and Franklin gave thanks. Unexpected warmth bubbled within me at his grasp, keeping my mind from the prayer. I muttered "amen" and readjusted my napkin.

"So, Aunt Belle, Seth tells me your friend, Ginnie, lost a pooch at her doggie hotel." Kevin buttered a roll. "You know about the missing dogs in Jackson, too. Fill me in on the one over there."

I stopped cutting my meat into chunks and looked at him. "Did Seth tell you about the missing dalmatians?"

Speaking around a mouthful of bread, he said, "No. What dalmatians?"

The story of Schotzie and the Clarence's dalmatians took us through a good portion of the meal. Kevin asked an occasional question along the way. "Sounds like more than coincidence to me." He nodded at Franklin. "That's why I brought Franklin in on this. He's a member of the Memphis area kennel club, and I thought he might shed some light on what's going on." He grinned. "Besides, I owe him dinner. I lost a bet."

Franklin laughed. "Some bet."

Seth raised an eyebrow. "What have you two got going on?"

"I told him the dog he bought wasn't worth training as a bird dog," Franklin said. "He was too skittish around noise."

"And Franklin was right," Kevin said. "After the first shot, that dog took off running. He's probably in Nashville by now."

We laughed. "You didn't get him back?" I asked.

"No. Didn't even try." Kevin shook his head. "He'll end up returning to Carl's farm down the road where we were shooting skeet. Carl said he'd call me, and I'll go pick him up then." He took a sip of tea. "Guess Mosey'll make a good watchdog instead of a bird dog. He can lie there and watch cars go by." He tipped his head in Franklin's direction. "He was the one who recognized Mosey's nerves. I bet him the dog would work, and he didn't. So I owe him dinner."

"Lupper," Seth said.

Kevin grinned. "Yeah, lupper."

Franklin looked puzzled.

"Don't ask," I said. "It's a family thing, hardly worth explaining." I scooped some gravy on my last bite of steak. "How do you know so much about dogs?"

"I raised them for a while then got too busy and had to give it up."

Seth said, "What business are you in?"

Kevin sipped his tea. "Franklin runs a landscaping business. He's the best in the county, in my opinion."

"Anyone who could tell a rose from a daisy would be good in your opinion," Seth piped up.

"Hey, now. My wife's gotten me to landscape our new yard, and Mother. . ." Kevin stopped short and looked at me.

"Your mom has such a green thumb." I smiled. "She can coax most any plant to grow."

The momentary tension broke. Kevin nodded a thanks in my direction.

I turned my attention to Franklin. The crinkles

around his eyes made them look merry. His watch glistened against his tan wrist, and his arms caught my attention. There was strength in him built with hard work. "Have you always been in landscaping?"

He nodded. "Guess you could say that. I have a degree in agriculture from Texas A&M, and it's been a stepping-stone for me." He chewed for a moment. "I farmed my dad's place a short while, raised some bird dogs and trained those, then formed my own business." He wiped his mouth with a napkin. "The landscaping won out, but I still enjoy watching and learning about dogs. I have a couple of my own I've turned into pets." He chuckled. "Lap dogs actually. Although Labradors don't fit in my lap well. They're pretty spoiled lying on the furniture and shedding on the carpet."

I smiled. "Guess your wife doesn't mind?"

"My wife didn't mind, rest her soul." His eyes clouded.

I dabbed my lips. "Oh, I'm sorry. Forgive me." I gazed into his mocha-colored eyes.

He patted my hand. "No way you could've known." His smile wavered. "She died of cancer about seven years ago. My dogs moved inside about then. Keeps the lonesomes away."

I remembered Ginnie's remark about the lonesomes. Seems like she and I weren't the only ones who suffered the syndrome.

Seth patted his stomach and reared back in his chair. "So, Mom, you said you wanted to tell us some information. Spill it."

I toyed with the straw's wrapper on the table while collecting my thoughts. "Well, I saw Harley today at the pet store."

"Harley Weston?" Kevin asked.

"Yes, the one and the same." I looked at Franklin. "I hate to bore you with my talk."

"Go ahead, Belle. Kevin asked for my input about the dogs."

I loved the way my name sounded on his lips. His even teeth appeared whiter against his tan, and his brow furrowed as he looked at me as though I were the only person in the room.

"Mom? What did Harley say?" Seth broke in.

"Oh, well, I asked him why someone would steal a dog." I looked at Franklin's hands. He had clean, manicured nails.

"And he said?" Impatience riddled Kevin's words.

I swung my gaze away from studying Franklin and looked at my nephew. "He gave me a good bit of information on what dognappers could do with the animals." I explained the conversation. "If there's as much money in dogs as Harley said, then I can see why they're stolen."

"Harley's right," Franklin said. "I've known people to spend up to sixty thousand dollars showing dogs."

"Sixty thousand? Why they must have more money than sense," I blurted.

"No." He smiled at me. "They know a good investment when they see it."

Chagrined, I said, "I guess I never thought of it in that manner. Ginnie said Violet Lester was going to breed Schotzie."

"She can make big bucks."

I thought about Harley's words. Big bucks in showing dogs.

Franklin spoke again. "Some pups go anywhere from five hundred to over a thousand, and there are usually several pups in a litter. Depends on the breed and the bloodlines. If they have good conformation, they go for more. There are a number of determining factors in pricing." Franklin shifted in his chair to face me. "We don't blink an eye at cattle sales. Dog breeding is no different." He leaned back. "In England there's a story of a man who sold his home for ransom money to get his dog returned."

"You have to be kidding." My eyes widened.

"Nope. It's a fact. These animals are expensive, yes, but they also become family to many. Dognapping in England has been rampant. You can find information on the Internet all the time about missing animals and the ransom that's been paid."

I snorted. "When there are so many other needs. . ."

He leaned forward and tapped the table, his eyes darkening in the restaurant's light. "I repeat, these animals become like family. If your kid was taken, there are not many stones you'd leave unturned to get him back. Same way with pets. People become attached and turn the animals into their children." He smiled. "If you haven't been in the world of very spoiled canines, you need to visit a dog show. It's a whole different experience." He paused. "Matter of fact, there's one in Memphis next weekend. Would you and your son like to go?"

I looked at Seth. "Would we?"

Seth smiled. "Sure we would. It might make a great newspaper story, and we can research more on missing pets." He tossed his napkin on his plate. "I appreciate the information, Mr. Jeffries."

"Franklin. Just call me Franklin." He smiled. "I'll get us free tickets. Kevin, you going?"

"Not this time, but thanks."

"Well, Franklin." Seth stood and extended his hand. "The *Jackson News* is glad to add another resource to our investigation."

Kevin stretched. "Aunt Belle, why do you want to get involved in all of this? Aren't you plenty busy as it is?"

"I'm busy, but my friends have lost their animals, and I'd like to be able to help find them." *And Pampered Pooch owes me money.*

Kevin grinned. "Then sleuth away, dear Auntie, but don't cross any lines or get into any trouble."

I frowned. "You're the second person today to make a reference to trouble. I resent that remark."

"No, Mom, you resemble that remark." Seth laughed. "You have been known to get involved and in over your head." He held my chair as I stood. "Let's see, for starters, there are the Gibsons down the street, who you just knew were growing weed in their hothouse—"

"How was I to know he'd started a plant business?" Heat crept into my cheeks. "Looked mighty suspicious to me."

Franklin looked at me. "Suspicious? A hothouse is suspicious?"

I ducked my head and felt the flush seep up my

ears. "Well, it was suspicious when they were out there at night with flashlights flickering. And then strange cars appeared on our street day and night."

Seth laughed. "Yes, and when Deputy Dawg checked it all out, he discovered they needed to harvest their crop after their regular work hours and get them to the growers while they were still fresh. Mr. Gibson's brothers were kind enough to pick up the loads and deliver them to nurseries in the wee hours." My son frowned in my direction. "Of course based on my mother's comments, the deputy went in armed and dangerous."

Kevin laughed. "Don's telling of this story eliminates the gun on his hip. Poor guy, keeping one step ahead of Aunt Belle can be difficult."

"Well, your mother seems to be a vigilant citizen protecting her neighborhood. I don't think there's anything wrong with that." Franklin patted my arm. A tingle ran up my spine.

"She's vigilant, all right. Not much gets by her." Seth looked at me. "Ready to go?"

I wasn't. I wanted to sit and talk with this man who'd been my champion. In a few short minutes, he'd made a favorable impression and given my feminine side a boost. I realized I was glad I'd taken an extra minute and freshened my makeup. Ginnie would be proud.

In the parking lot, Seth and Kevin chatted. Franklin leaned against his truck and asked me about my job.

"I'm into room-scaping I guess you'd say." I chuckled.

He crinkled his brow. "Room-scaping? That's a

new one on me."

I trailed a finger across the dust on the hood of his truck, and a clean streak appeared. "I own a cleaning service. Belle's Feather Duster. You make beautiful yards; I make clean rooms."

We both laughed.

"Well, yours is a service I might need to employ. This dirty truck is an example of my housekeeping abilities." He scratched his chin. "Working full-time, I don't pay much attention to what needs doing."

"Just call. I'll be there." I blushed after the words escaped my lips.

"I think I'll do that, Miz Feather Duster. Soon. Real soon." He nodded in my direction, said good-bye to the boys, and climbed into his truck. He started the engine and then rolled down the window. "We have the dog show to look forward to, don't forget." With a wink, he put the truck in gear.

I nodded. Forget? How could I forget? His warm eyes and wide grin made my heart feel young again. Lupper had been great.

7

The following morning a phone call came from Ginnie during breakfast. I told her what Harley had said.

"Research labs?" she squeaked. "Schotzie could've gone to some research lab? Oh, Belle, I feel worse now."

"Honey, we don't know that for sure." I toyed with a piece of cereal swimming in milk, searching my mind for words of comfort. "Schotzie's too gorgeous. Harley indicated purebred dogs don't go to labs."

"Now that makes me feel better." She sighed. "Schotzie's at some mill, grinding out puppies. I may be sick."

"I just thought I'd tell you what I know." I poked the bran flake again, but it wouldn't stay submerged.

She paused. "I know you may think I'm overreacting, but I wish I could find that dog." I heard her sip a drink.

Me too. In six weeks I'll face the bank officer. Will there be money in the kitty? I shoved the bowl across the table and kneaded my forehead. Another thought popped into my brain. "I didn't know Mel had worked for you."

"Yes, he did."

"Need me to bring his paycheck this way?" I was meddling but oh so curious.

Ginnie sighed. "I've already mailed it."

"He's beginning a handyman business. Did you know?"

No response.

"What? I guess Belinda told you—"

"She mentioned it, but I won't be using his service. Ever." Her clipped words let me know she was aggravated. "I don't want to be around him after the last visit. He embarrassed me. In front of Violet Lester, no less."

I propped my hand on my hip. "You didn't tell me this story."

Ginnie's voice was tinged with anger. "Belle, that man was flirting with me. He's winked at me several times before when he'd been by to see Mitch. Made a pass at me in the grocery store one day." She huffed. "This time, he actually put his arm around my shoulders. And who should walk in but—"

"Violet Lester," I groaned.

"Yep. I was furious. And let him know." She paused. "When he walked outside, Violet told me of his reputation. She wasn't very nice, either. I believe Mel heard her."

"Oh my." I swiveled the salt shaker and pictured pretty Belinda. "I thought he and Belinda were the perfect couple. I'm amazed."

"Perfect couples seldom are. I mailed his check and am glad only Belinda brings in their beagle."

Mel, angry at Ginnie and Violet, too. Now there's a motive for snatching that particular pooch. I barely heard Ginnie's comments about the upcoming women's breakfast at church, trying to imagine where Mel would've taken the dog.

She broke into my reverie with a question. "So

what else is new?"

"I had dinner with Seth." My eyes brightened. "And I met a man."

"What? What man?"

I had her attention now. "Kevin joined us for dinner last night and brought along a friend of—"

"Oh, you met another young man."

"Of course he's young." I smiled. "A veritable spring chicken." I snickered. "He's our age."

Ginnie snorted. "Now this I have to hear. Tell me more."

"Landscaper, college degree, trains dogs." I dished out all the details, leaving out the part where I gawked at Franklin too much. "He was incredibly good-looking and interesting."

"Belle, in all the years I've known you, I've never heard you go on this way. Especially about a man." She gave a silly laugh. "Think you're coming alive again, girl?"

I could feel the heat rise in my face and remembered the tingling sensation from Franklin's touch. My ears burned. "Stop it, Ginnie. He's just a really nice man. I liked him." *I liked him a lot.* Warning signs flashed and my chest tightened. I'd liked Peter a lot after meeting him the first time, too.

She heaved a sigh. "It would be so amazing to have someone interesting to talk with. Might even be nice to have a dinner partner once in a while, don't you think?" She paused then continued with a lilt. "I hope that's what this will become for you."

I chuckled. "Think you're getting a little ahead of

yourself, my dear. I only met the man and made some casual observations."

"Methinks thou dost protest too much."

"Go on, Shakespeare." Cradling the phone on my shoulder, I carried my cereal bowl to the sink and turned on the water, adding dishwashing liquid. "So what plans do you have for today?" I slid dishes into the water and soaped them.

"Not a thing. Just work with the dogs. But. . ." she moaned, "the claims adjustor called, and they are going to send someone out to look at the kennel."

"Why?" I rinsed the bowl and a glass and placed them on a dish towel to dry.

"They need to check the security to see if it meets the company standards now. I don't know, some red tape." Ice clinked in a glass. "No telling how long it will be before I get money to pay for Schotzie." She groaned. "Oh, Belle, I just know my business has fallen off because of Donetta and Violet. Donetta told the whole league group we didn't have enough security on our property. I heard that from Sukey's daughter. Violet's telling everyone it's my fault the dog is missing. Maddie Simpson told me when I ran into her at the grocery that Violet's spitting mad. And she's calling me careless."

"Careless?" A plate slid from my hand and almost crashed to the floor. "Ginnie, you're obsessive about those dogs. You don't have a careless attitude in you. And people who matter don't believe Violet or Donetta. Their attitudes precede them." I wiped my hands and leaned against the counter. "Besides, they don't know all the details. Like bubblegum on camera lenses. I noticed the newspaper article didn't mention that detail."

"Yes, Seth said Sheriff Connors suggested leaving that part out." She sighed. "Seth did a good job, but still. . .it's negative news."

"Let's think. How can we turn business around?" *And turn it around quickly*, I thought. I crossed one arm over the other and nuzzled the phone closer to my ear. I heard her sniffle and forced my tone to brighten. "You can advertise a special rate again, maybe a coupon to gain some new clients."

"Maybe I'm not geared for business." Her voice held a near whine. "Especially a business on your property."

"Ginnie, don't give up. Pampered Pooch is a good idea. God didn't lead you this far to let you down. And we prayed over the land lease, remember? It's going to work out."

"Arabelle Blevins, ever the optimist."

"Not always. But I know we prayed about Pampered Pooch, so we have to trust, don't we?"

"Humph. I know." Ginnie grew silent for a moment. "But, Belle, it's my reputation on the line here."

And my money. "Have you thought about advertising at the dog show in Memphis?"

"Yes, I've already sent some pamphlets to the organizers. There will be an area for local information, and they assured me that my brochures will be displayed."

"Well, I can certainly check that out."

"What?"

"I plan on going to the show. Seth and I discussed it on the way home." My mind raced to Franklin. I hoped we'd see him—he wouldn't just send Seth tickets, would he? "Want to come with us?" I turned around and rinsed the suds from the sink and wiped it with a sponge. "Maybe you can meet Franklin."

"No, I won't be able to attend." She laughed. "Get Seth to shoot a picture of you and the hunk so I can see him."

"Right. If we even see him." The phone began to slide from my shoulder. "Gotta run, sweetie. So much to do." I heard her good-bye and grabbed the receiver, punching the OFF button. It rang before I placed it in the cradle.

"Belle, this is Franklin Jeffries, Kevin's friend."

My ears heated up again, and my pulse raced. "Why hello, Franklin, how are you?"

"I wanted to firm up plans for the dog show, so I got your number from Kevin. I hope that's okay." He paused. "Since you and your son are so interested in what's been going on, I thought you'd like an insider's perspective. I could meet you and show you around."

My heart did a happy dance. He was going to be there. "We'd like that very much." We agreed on a meeting place. I closed my eyes after he hung up and visualized his manicured hands holding mine as we prayed. Such strength. Despite my protests, I felt giddy. A foreign feeling for sure.

Seth, his photographer, and I arrived at the Memphis fairgrounds early on Saturday morning. Motor homes filled the parking lot, air conditioners rumbling. Harley had been right—the handlers traveled in style. We picked up the tickets Franklin had arranged at the will-call window and entered the coliseum. A swell of people and dogs filled the area. Kibble and other unidentified smells greeted my nose. Ginnie wasn't in charge here, and the odor was overpowering.

Barks and growls, blow dryers, and clanking metal roared in my ears. Rows and rows of dog-filled cages and grooming stations lined one side of the arena. People young and old sprawled in lawn chairs, ice chests and snacks beside them, and hovered over their pets.

The grooming stations had been set up to ready the animals for show. Each station held a table and enough equipment to fashion a beauty parlor. Handlers busily shuffled dogs from pens to tables.

White-tented booths around the edges of the enormous room advertised an array of products for dogs and their owners.

Scanning the crowd, I looked for Franklin. He'd be hard to spot in the jumble.

Seth touched my elbow. "This way, Mom. The note in the ticket envelope said we're to meet him by the American Kennel Club information desk."

Seth and I wound our way in and around dogs and people. At the AKC desk, the photographer set up his camera and snapped away as Seth interviewed the woman in charge. I fanned some of the local advertisements and spotted Pampered Pooch brochures. With a peek at management, I pulled them to the forefront of the table and arranged them nicely.

I felt a tap on my shoulder and turned to face Franklin. "Hey, there."

"Belle, sorry I'm late." His magnetic grin lit up his face, and I smiled back.

"Not a problem. We just got here. Seth's already taking notes for his story." I pointed to the arena. "This is amazing. I've never seen so many dogs and people all in one place."

"It is a large show. Let me give you a tour if that's okay with your son." Franklin stepped toward Seth, hand extended. "May I borrow your mom for a bit?"

They shook hands, and we agreed to meet back at the AKC desk by noon. The crowd nearby was so thick that we almost got separated. Franklin reached for my hand to guide me. I liked the feeling of his fingers intertwined with mine. Excitement mingled with caution tugged at my heart.

"Over here are the exhibits." We threaded our way down a crowded aisle. The brightly lit booths held collars, dog beds, chew toys, and rows of other goods. Everything from flea powder to pooper-scoopers were available for purchase. T-shirts hung on end caps depicted all sorts of dog breeds and various dog-lover axioms. A pimply-faced teenager manned a table with brochures for pet health insurance. I picked one up to check the premiums and wondered if Violet had kept up the health policy on Schotzie. I shook my head when the boy offered me a pen to fill out information. I didn't even have health insurance; I sure wasn't in need of it for a dog.

We strolled on. A little girl held a poodle on a leash at the first booth. The sign said PET DELI. I leaned over to check the merchandise. Tiny slices of liver? I wrinkled my nose. Foil bags filled with pepperoni pieces sat on the bottom row. I watched the miniature dog sniff at packages as the child held them to his nose. At the fourth bag, the dog began to lick the cover, and the young shopper seemed pleased. She handed her money to the cashier.

"He must've liked that flavor." Franklin chuckled.

"I never knew so much existed for pet comfort." I scanned the area.

"You ain't seen nothing yet." He pulled me in another direction. "Look at this group."

I strolled to the booth's opening. A man dressed in scrubs leaned over a collie lying on a table. He positioned the dog's outstretched legs and then proceeded to knead the dog's side. The collie's eyes were closed, and I'm sure she had a grin on her muzzle. I leaned back to look at the banner: MASSAGE THERAPIST.

"Lassie probably strained her muscles during the agility runs," Franklin said.

I shook my head. "If we cover this whole arena, I may stop back in for a foot massage."

Franklin laughed and waved his hand at another booth. "Or a pup could be experiencing too much stress. Then they could receive help here."

A sign clipped to the end of the booth announced PET PSYCHIC. A heavy-set woman sat knee-to-knee talking to a man with a furrowed brow. A large dog lay at their feet. I couldn't hear the conversation but had to cover my mouth to keep from laughing.

I grabbed Franklin's elbow and whispered, "You have to be kidding me. What on earth could she be saying?"

"Maybe Fido is unhappy with his sleeping arrangements." Franklin grinned. "Or maybe he needs more understanding from his owner."

"People really believe this?" I raised my eyebrows as Franklin pointed at the smaller print on the sign: DOG DOES NOT NEED TO BE PRESENT FOR READING.

Franklin said, "Well, that's good to know. She works long distance without the pet present."

I picked up a brochure from the display. My mouth dropped open. "Two hundred dollars an hour for a home visit?" I stared at the woman before we continued down the row.

He nodded. "This is big business, Belle. People believe a lot of strange things." He sighed. "Wish the whole world was full of believers in the right thing; then we'd have a dog chapel. I'd sure rather have that than a psychic." He took my elbow. "Let's go look at some dogs." We ambled along looking at the vast array of sweatshirts, sweaters for dogs, and glittery leads before we reached the open area of pens.

Wandering one aisle, I stopped and watched as a petite woman groomed a Newfoundland. With a struggle, she lifted the huge animal onto the grooming table and hitched his head in a noose. He must've weighed close to a hundred pounds. I thought of the Newfoundland Seth said was stolen. No small feat.

The dog had been shampooed earlier in a bathing

area and begun to air dry. She pulled out a drier and blew his hair completely dry. The forceful breeze was not hot. I surmised she didn't need to overheat the dog's skin. *That'd be one huge scalded dog.*

With a fine-toothed comb, she curried every inch of his body, clipping stray hairs, fluffing out others. Fuzz covered her smock and her blond hair. She blew her bangs out of her face and glanced in our direction.

I spoke, "He's a beautiful dog."

"Thanks. He's here for his final points." She smiled and patted the dog's back. "I think we'll ace this one; the competition is pretty weak." The dog swiveled his head at her words. "See, he knows, too."

We both chuckled.

"Good luck," Franklin said.

Following the long row, we passed dogs of differing breeds. "I didn't realize how many kinds of dogs God created," I said.

Franklin smiled. "Yes, He was pretty busy. This is an all-breed show where many breeds compete. Sometimes we have specialty shows with just one breed." We walked on. "Showing dogs is a great sport. It's a competition combined with seeing beautiful animals."

"I am amazed." Two pens caught my attention. Squished-faced pugs stared out. I wanted to tug on their noses and help straighten their faces.

Sharp barking caught my attention. I turned and saw Jared Clarence jerking a dog's leash, tugging it down an aisle. Aggravation colored his face. When he saw me, his eyes widened.

I raised a hand. "Jared."

He startled at my call, bent, tucked the small dog under his arm, and scurried the other direction. Before I could follow, he disappeared from view. What was he doing at this dog show?

Franklin's voice broke into my thoughts.

"We have dog shows to evaluate breeding stock." Franklin pointed to one pug. "This is a good-looking dog. A dog's conformation, or overall appearance and structure, is an indication of its ability to produce quality puppies. And as we said, it's a business."

He gestured toward one tiny dog shivering on the next table. "Don't understand this one too well."

I spotted the skinny, hairless Chihuahua, ribs showing, a fluff of a tail the only hair. I wrinkled my nose. "No, that one isn't my favorite, but I bet the owner feels differently." I glanced over my shoulder. No sign of Jared.

"You're getting it now." He squeezed my shoulder. "These are more than pets; to many they are family. A pet can become more important than anyone else, because he gives unconditional love."

I watched the owner caress the odd dog. She gathered him into her arms and cooed into his ear. "Yes, I can see how that happens." My thoughts strayed to Lauren and her Chihuahua. I wondered if she were here and if she'd cross Seth's path.

We neared the center of the arena where short white picket fencing formed ten circles. "Those are the show rings." Franklin found us two folding chairs in front of a ring. "Let's watch a round, and I'll explain it some more." He held out the chair for me. "The judges will examine the dogs and give them ribbons. He bestows the awards according to how closely each dog compares to his mental image of the 'perfect' dog in that breed."

"Sounds pretty subjective." I settled my purse in my lap and swung my gaze around the area looking for a teenager with a guilty expression.

"Well, the AKC has an official standard that describes the characteristics for which he looks. Those characteristics explain what allows the dog to perform the function for which it was bred. Each judge is an expert in the breed they judge."

My eyes met his. "So he knows what he's looking for."

"Exactly. He'll go over each dog with his hands to feel its muscles, bones, and coat texture. See if it conforms to the breed's standards. He'll watch its gait as the handler trots it around the ring. Then he'll award ribbons."

"Hmm." I watched a line of handlers bring dogs into the center aisle between the tiny show rings.

While we waited, Franklin talked a bit about his show days. "I enjoyed the dogs and the shows for a long while, but after my wife died, I gave it up. It's a lot of work, and I didn't want to continue alone. So I moved to Memphis." He ran one hand over his chin, and I thought it was an adorable habit. "I needed a change. My parents had been gone a while, and with no children, I uprooted and landed here."

"It's a good spot." I smiled. *And I'm glad you landed nearby.*

A man entered the show ring, his navy blazer, tie, and khaki pants setting him apart from the crowd.

Franklin lifted his chin in that direction. "The judge. Getting to his position isn't easy. You have to be well experienced and have bred and raised four champions. Takes a long time. Judges come up through the ranks after traveling and showing dogs for over twelve years."

A new admiration shot through my mind. The salt-and-pepper-haired judge waved at a woman who led in a dog.

"A beagle. My neighbor has one," I murmured.

"Yes. Now the handler will follow the directions of the judge so he can best examine the animal's conformation. Watch."

The judge waved, and the woman trotted her dog around the ring. They stopped in front of him. The woman positioned her dog, pulling each leg to straighten it, clasping his muzzle, offering a treat. The judge skimmed his hands down the dog's back, lifted its head, examined its mouth, then stepped back. With one hand on the dog's chin, the judge's eyes ran up and down the length of the animal. He nodded, and the woman and dog trotted around the ring again. Another nod and she stopped and stood on one end of the circle. Not a word had been spoken.

Another contestant entered the ring, and the process was followed once more. Three more beagles competed. As the last one took his position, the judge nodded to the first woman. She trotted her dog around the ring, and the others ran behind. I watched the judge. His eyes probed each animal as it passed. He took a step forward once they stopped and reexamined the animals. Finally, he backed off, pointed a finger at one, two, three, and four dogs.

Franklin whispered, "He just awarded first, second, third, and fourth."

"That was fast." I thought about all the preparation it took for just a few minutes' time. "It hardly seems worth the effort." I watched as the ribbons were handed out.

"Again, winning makes points for the dog, and points make a champion. You own a champion, the breeding costs increase. You charge more for a puppy and for stud fees. It's all math." He gripped my hand. "You want something to drink?"

I nodded, my heart in my throat as our fingers connected. "Water would be great. I'm going across the aisle." I pointed toward the ladies' room. "Meet you back here?"

He squeezed my fingers and headed to a concession stand.

I veered from the direction of the restroom and retraced my steps, weaving in and out of dog pens to the point I'd last seen Jared. An open garage door leading to a loading dock spilled sunlight into the arena. I trekked down the slanted ramp. RVs and several pickup trucks sat parallel with the building. I stood on tiptoe and examined the area. No sign of him.

"Excuse me," I spoke to a woman entering the ramp holding a fluffy white dog. "Are dalmatians in this arena?"

The woman jerked her head around and stared down her nose at me. "My expertise is with bichons frises. I'd have no idea about larger animals."

"Thank you." I whirled around and continued on my original route, scanning dog pens and people's faces. Still no bubblegum-chewing kid.

One circle brought me back to the white picket fences. I'd lost my seat, so Franklin stood and gave me his.

"Everything okay?" His mocha eyes scrutinized me.

"Absolutely."

He handed me an ice cold water bottle. We watched the next round of beagles, this time females. The same procedure produced winners. After three rounds, the top dog of each entered the ring.

"Best of breed." He nodded in the ring's direction. "The winner here will compete later in best of show."

We applauded politely as winners were announced and removed from the ring. I fastened my gaze on a dog as he left and laughed as it paused by a post and lifted its leg. "Well, that's not nice in public."

"Didn't you notice?" He pointed. "All the posts have litter sprinkled around them for just such a purpose."

I looked, and sure enough, sawdust lay in circles around the post areas. "They think of everything." The dog show idea tickled me. "This is a whole new world." I glanced at my watch. "I think we need to meet up with Seth in just a few minutes."

As I stood, another woman grabbed the back of the folding chair. Seating was limited, and she appeared anxious. I stepped out of her way, and she scooted in, eyes on the ring. I figured she must be someone's mom to have that much intensity.

"Franklin, do you suppose dalmatians are being shown?"

"We can check the program." He rifled through pages. "I don't see them listed." He studied my face. "Was there a particular reason you wanted to see them? Like looking for missing dogs from Jackson?" He pursed his lips. "Belle, your son mentioned your penchant for mysteries. You aren't sleuthing, are you?"

I gave a nervous laugh. "No, of course not." I really hadn't been. Just looking for one of the Clarence boys. "I wondered if my friends were here. Let's go find the others."

Seth and his photographer leaned against the AKC counter. When my son saw us approach, he met us partway. "Franklin, the president of your area kennel club was looking for you. Did he find you?"

Franklin shook his head. "Michael? What did he want?"

A voice from behind answered. "Susanne's Yorkie has been stolen."

I wheeled around to see a skinny man lope up.

"Security's working the doors in a search, and her dad wanted to report it here in case someone saw something suspicious." He motioned to a man approaching.

The distraught man ran a hand over his balding pate. "Susanne left Lady in the pen and went to eat." His lips pressed together in a grim line. "She knows not to let that dog out of her sight."

"Gordon, she's just a kid." Franklin reached over and touched his shoulder.

"A kid who had a dog to show," he snapped. "She knew better." He balled his hands into fists. "If I could get my hands on whoever. . ."

Jared's face flashed through my mind. But what did I know about the kid? His family had show dogs. I hesitated to point a finger just because he chewed bubblegum and his freckles had brightened when I called his name.

Franklin's soothing voice caught at my heart. "This anger isn't good, Gordon. Susanne must really be upset." He seemed to realize how tender a child's feelings were.

"Well, I wanted to put the word out so others would be more careful. We don't need a run of disappearing dogs." Gordon motioned to the clerk at the AKC table.

Seth said, "Seems like we already have a number of missing animals."

Gordon faced him. "Who are you?"

"Seth Blevins, *Jackson News*."

"A reporter?" Gordon's eyes brightened. "That's what we need, publicity, to get the word out about our Yorkie."

Franklin stepped forward. "It's not just your dog, Gordon. There's been a rash of thefts, it seems. Seth is investigating the losses, and his mother, Belle, came to find out more about the kennel world." He introduced me.

"I'm sorry about your dog," I said. "I know your daughter must feel awful."

Gordon seemed to deflate. "She does." He ran his hand over his head again. "And I don't think I helped by exploding and walking off."

Franklin grasped his elbow, guided him to the end of the booth area, and motioned for us to follow.

"Gordon, we'll report this to security, but first, let's pray for Susanne and her dog." He bowed his head and asked God to bless the girl and dog.

Tears filled my eyes. What a kind man. A real one-of-a-kind man. Maybe he could pray for Pampered Pooch and my tax money.

8

Monday morning, the alarm clock startled me from a Franklin-filled dream. I groaned and snuggled deeper under the down comforter, content to daydream and run bits of footage through my memory. Sitting behind a cuddly couple in Sunday's church service had only welled up the loneliness, and thoughts of a brown-haired gentleman kept me from concentrating. *I wonder what church he attends.*

I rolled to one side and slid from the bed. "Enough. I'm not a teenager. This is foolish." I frowned in the mirror as I brushed my teeth. *But he's such a very nice man. I wish. . .* I rinsed and peered at my reflection. "What in the world would I wish for?"

Heaving a sigh, I trudged to the bedroom and pulled on my standard cleaning uniform—a pair of jeans and a T-shirt. My tennis shoes lay in the kitchen, so I padded down the hall in bare feet. It was too hot for socks this morning.

I plunked two pieces of bread in the toaster and grabbed a cold soda. After a swallow, I opened the front door and gathered in the *Jackson News*. An above-the-fold picture of the dog show captured my attention. There I stood beside Franklin, grinning at the hairless Chihuahua. I had no clue Seth's photographer had been nearby. I held the paper at arm's length. We made a fetching couple.

"At least Ginnie will see the mystery man." I chuckled.

No sooner had the words left my mouth than the phone rang. I peered at the ID display and snatched up the receiver. "Hey, Ginnie. I had you on my mind."

"I'm surprised a celebrity like you answers the phone," she said.

The toast popped up, and I sat at the table to spread grape jelly, a smile tugging at my lips. "You saw the picture."

"I did." The newspaper rattled. "I think you make a dahling couple."

"The dog and me?"

"Belle." She laughed. "This guy's handsome. Where did you say he was from?"

"I didn't." I sipped from the can. "But he's originally from Nashville and moved to Memphis when his wife died. He has no children. He has his own landscaping company." I paused. "Did I leave out anything?" I chewed a bite of toast then took a drink.

"His pedigree." She snickered.

I snorted and cola spewed. "Pedigree?"

"From whence do his people come?" Her affected Southern accent brought on a gale of laughter. "You know how society is. You must have good blue bloodlines."

"The only bloodlines I know about belong to dogs. I learned most of that Saturday." I wiped the counter and my face with a paper towel. "You've made me splatter my shirt."

"Sorry. Didn't learn anything about dognappers, did you?"

"You know, Ginnie, I saw one of the Clarence boys at the show. Do you know if they got their dogs back?"

"Haven't heard. And Therese called me about Schotzie. She never mentioned traveling to Memphis."

"Maybe Jared was there helping a friend." *A thief friend? I'd call Theresa myself.*

Ginnie interrupted my thoughts. "Go change and call me later if you have time for lunch. Where do you work today?"

"In Jackson. The Millers." I held my shirt out to dry. "I won't have time for lunch; it's a pretty big job. I'll check in tonight." We said our good-byes, and I slid on my shoes. "Bloodlines." I shook my head and laughed. "Ginnie is a nut." Rummaging in my purse for my cell phone, I dialed Theresa's number and listened to it ring. When the answering machine began, I hung up. This wasn't a question for an answering machine. Actually, how did you ask a client if her precious kid was a dognapper?

Finishing my breakfast, I wiped off the counter with a spit and a promise then headed out the door. Mel had the Jeep in good running order by the time I'd returned from Memphis Saturday. He'd put a new whatchamacallit on the carburetor that hadn't cost much, and the motor purred as I sat in traffic. Gratitude for God's provision filled my heart; then it went into a rat-a-tat as I thought of Mel. How far would he go for revenge? Violet's known fondness for gossip could lead him to retaliate against her. Then again, Ginnie had rebuffed his flirtatious attempts. Sitting at a red light, I whacked the steering wheel. *Mel, my helpful neighbor? A cheater?*

Traffic thickened as I drove in the outskirts of

Jackson. The town had grown by leaps and bounds in the years since I'd moved to Trennan. New housing and stores dotted the area, changing the familiar landscape. Our old church looked weathered and worn in the midst of strip malls and service stations. Today the grief pang I usually experienced when I drove by didn't slam into me as hard. Maybe healing had begun. I smiled. Mocha eyes might have something to do with that process.

Betty Miller had her front door wide open as I parked by the curb. Her two-story, yellow house sat back on a blanket of green lawn. A pebble-covered sidewalk bordered by colorful flower beds full of petunias and impatiens ran to the porch. She waited on the swing, newspaper in hand and a grin on her face, her red wavy ponytail ruffled in the breeze.

"Well, well, do tell." She flapped the paper at me. "Who is this guy, and where did you meet him?"

I laughed and bounced up the steps. "Mystery man." We walked indoors. "I went with Seth to cover the dog show, and we ran into a friend." I tapped the picture. "Franklin Jeffries. He knows Kevin and showed us around the grounds." I plopped my purse on her kitchen counter. "Anything extra you need today?"

"Is that all you're going to tell me, Belle? I expected some juicy gossip." Betty planted one hand on her hip, her brown eyes twinkling.

"Nothing to tell." I turned to the sink and ran some water then glanced her way. "Yet." I giggled.

"Oh boy. I like the sound of that." She slid in beside me and squeezed my shoulders, a waft of perfume hovering in the air. "It's about time. You deserve some happiness."

"I don't know about deserve, but I might take some."

A crease formed between her eyes, and she said, "I think God's children deserve the best. And you came out on the raw end of your marriage." She tossed a napkin in the trash. "So I'm expecting a blessing."

"Thanks, Betty." My nose stung. She'd been one of the faithful few in Peter's congregation. Others didn't know what to say to the outcast wife. It had definitely been a time of loneliness and uncertainty and taking sides. I never figured out how they set the rules so Peter and I had sides. My sister-in-law's unforgiving face floated through my mind, and I bit my trembling lip. I mentally nudged the feeling away.

Water covered the bowls sitting in the sink, and I sloshed them around, scrubbing a few with the sponge. "So, I repeat, anything extra for me to do?"

"Now that you mention it. . ." She scooted to the pantry and returned with a can of soup. "Mark is home with a bad cold and is going to be hungry. Would you mind feeding him while I'm gone?"

"Of course not." I set the can on the counter. "Does he have a fever? Will he need any medicine?" I usually didn't nurse clients to health, but Mark was such a sweet teenager. An oxymoron for many of my clients' kids. I frowned at the thought of Jared's insolence.

"He has Tylenol by his bed and can take two about twelve-thirty." Betty picked up her keys. "I hate to ask you to be a nursemaid, Belle."

"It's okay. Seriously, I don't mind." I nodded. "I remember what it was like when Seth was a sick teen, so I'll tread carefully."

Betty laughed. "He'll be in bed or on his computer playing a game. He's missing school, but I've allowed him that much room to move about." She opened the door. "Thanks again. See you in a bit." Her ponytail swished as she turned back. "And the new guy? He's mighty good-looking. Hope he's a keeper." She winked and left.

I smiled. A keeper? I wiped the kitchen counter. I thought Peter was my keeper. With a sigh, I tossed the dishrag in the sink.

Before I began work in earnest, I peeked in at Mark. He was sound asleep. I'd start cleaning in the kitchen, the farthest from his room, so I wouldn't wake him. I hummed a tune while I loaded the dishwasher. Yes, Franklin was mighty good-looking, but Peter had been too. I wasn't sure where this friendship would lead, but it would be a cautious one.

By the time I'd finished his parents' bathroom and started the bedroom, Mark wandered my way. "Hey, Miss Belle."

His nasal voice startled me. "Morning, Mark. Feeling any better?" I pulled the sheets up and straightened the pillows.

"I think so." He sneezed. "A little."

"I'll fix you some soup when you're ready to eat." I smoothed the edge of the freshly made bed. "Do you need a drink or anything?"

"Oh, yeah, that'd be great." He sniffled.

"I'll bring you some orange juice. How's that?" I placed my hand on his elbow and propelled him toward his room. "You climb in bed and rest. I'll be right back."

Climbing upstairs, I heard the rush of his feet as he scrambled across his room. I opened the door and saw him slide into bed. A computer screen saver danced lights across the ceiling.

"Your mom said you could play games." I nodded at the monitor. "If you feel up to it."

He took his juice and downed it in a few swallows. "I might in a minute. The computer's booting up." He frowned. "I wasn't sure if you'd be mad because I was playing."

"No, if your mom said it was okay, I don't mind one bit." I fluffed his pillow as he leaned over to place the glass on the nightstand. "I'll be near if you need anything."

"Thank you, Miss Belle."

Betty had purchased two vacuum cleaners for her home before I came to work there: upstairs and downstairs. I removed one from the upstairs closet and swept it across the plush carpet. As the swaths of pile raised, I thought of Franklin and wondered if he mowed grass during the day. A secret smile played across my lips. I couldn't believe how often my mind ran to his activities.

Scrubbing the bathroom floor, I reviewed my savings account. Would there be enough to cover what I would need in June? Oh, Schotzie, why did you disappear? Where are you? Besides the money, I'd become concerned about the dog. The pet owners at the dog show had been wrapped around their animals. I knew Linda felt the same way about her pup.

Close to noon, I warmed a bowl of chicken noodle soup, poured juice, gathered some saltine crackers, and fixed a tray. I carried it to Mark's room. He sat at the computer desk, one leg propped up on the chair, the other dangling, his hair sticking up in all directions.

"Lunchtime." I slid the tray on the desk. "What game are you playing?"

He bit into a cracker. "Not a game."

Pictures filled his computer monitor. "Looks like snapshots. Do you have a photo album on there?" I turned for the Tylenol and shook out two.

He slurped a spoonful of noodles and smiled. "Sort of." He pointed with his spoon. "This is a neat Web site called MySpace."

I handed him the medicine and stepped closer. "Wow. This really is an album." Rows of pictures bordered the right side of the screen, teenagers of all ages. Phrases filled the other side, but the writing was too small for me to read. "Who are all these kids?"

"My friends." Mark spoke with his mouth full. I waited while he swallowed the tablets. "People on the Net. It's really cool."

I straightened. "I hope you're careful about who you meet and what you say." I reached for his wastebasket and set it in the hall then straightened the covers on his bed.

"Oh, yeah. I mean, we just talk about music and stuff. No big deal."

"Hmm, that's good. Sounds like fun." I picked up dirty clothes to drop in the laundry and tossed tennis shoes in his closet.

"Want to see my site?" He clicked the mouse a few times. "Here I am." He slurped more soup.

I walked to the desk. A young Mark flashed on the screen, a photo from earlier in the school year. Under it were pictures from his youth group trip to the lake, his dog and cat, and a music album cover. Several friends were listed under his name. I tapped the screen. "Do you know those people? Do they live around here?"

He chuckled. "No, Miss Belle. They're cyber friends." He clicked on a girl's face. "She's really hot. But she lives across the country." His eyes gleamed. "Sometimes she sends me an IM."

"A what?"

"You know, instant message. You chat with people in real time." His look indicated how old-fashioned he found me. "I'm chatting now with a guy from church."

Mark clicked the bottom of the screen and a box popped up. The caption read: *Hey, we did it!*

"Why isn't he in school?"

Mark sniffled. "I think Jared caught the same cold I did."

I bent to peek at the IM square. A dalmatian's face was in the IM box. "Jared Clarence?"

"Yes, ma'am, it's Jared." He minimized the IM.

"Well, just be careful online." Those canned words had been on the nightly news, though I didn't know exactly what they meant.

He shrugged. "I will. I'm not stupid."

He might as well have shouted, "Clueless, old lady," because I was.

I heard the front door close and Betty's call. I turned to leave, wastebasket in hand. "See you later, Mark. Hope you feel better."

He nodded. "Thanks." He popped the last cracker in his mouth and muffled, "And thanks for lunch."

"You bet." I closed his bedroom door. Mark was a nice kid. Cyberspace. There's more and more to learn from the Internet. I shrugged and rolled my head to unravel knots in my neck. I was exhausted and ready to go home.

Betty's arrival meant my exit.

9

I was dog-tired by evening. After work, I watered my yard and pulled some weeds from the flower beds. Tonight, as I braced my back with one hand and climbed the porch steps, I praised my decision to hire a neighbor boy to cut the grass.

I dropped to a porch chair. The evening breeze cooled my damp T-shirt and unraveled tension from my shoulders. Purple and white phlox spread across the oval flower bed near the street, and yellow jonquils and petunias danced against the wind near the house. My yard didn't rival Mel's, but it was pretty. He stepped outside at my thought and called, "Hello."

I managed a smile in response.

"Hey, Belle. Flowers look pretty good."

"Pretty good. Ha! You'd think we were competing."

Rolling up a hose, he shook his head. "No more competition for this old fellow. Too tired." His morose tone caught my attention. He tossed the hose in the garage. Definitely out of character for the neat-freak Mel. His eyes darted to the front door. "Talk to you later. The wife's calling." He slid the garage door closed.

I felt awkward talking to him after Ginnie's story. Mel's friendship dated back to my teen years. I wasn't sure I wanted to know about his marriage. Seems he'd crossed Belinda once again. I leaned my head against the back of the chair and closed my eyes. I hated that he had to worry about money at this point in life. *Money.* Mel's strong arms and wiry frame could boost him to a window ledge. And he'd had a confrontation with Ginnie and heard Violet's comments.

I shook my head. Everyone in my life was becoming a suspect.

I surveyed the yard again and tapped a finger on the chair. Maybe I needed a landscaper's help with my flower beds. A flush crept up my face. *Belle, you need help all right.*

Shaking my head, I stood and rubbed the small of my back then stomped dirt from my tennis shoes. I slid them off by the door and tossed my gardening gloves in the laundry room.

After a quick shower, I threw on a nightgown and robe. In the kitchen, I opened the pantry on a food quest. Nothing caught my fancy, and cooking wasn't an option. Even nuking a frozen dinner seemed a pain, so a peanut butter sandwich and some chips served as dinner. I munched in front of the TV watching the news.

A short clip on the missing Yorkie and other dogs played across the screen. I picked up the remote and hit the volume button to hear Gordon tell about his daughter's loss. The camera zoomed in on Susanne as she stood beside him, tears tracing down her cheeks. I felt bad for the little girl. The reporter gave a brief rundown on missing pedigreed pets in the area and urged viewers to become responsible pet owners. A spokesperson from the Memphis kennel club gave a Web site address that had tips on keeping animals safe. I licked my fingers, grabbed a pencil, and jotted the information down on my napkin.

Once the news ended, I carried my plate to the kitchen and used the small vacuum to clean up chip crumbs. I plopped on the couch and channel surfed for a few minutes, but nothing caught my attention. I felt restless. I picked up the napkin with the Web site and traipsed into the extra bedroom to turn on the computer. Seth had insisted I have his old machine, and though surfing the Net was new to me, I had read his newspaper stories online and e-mailed friends from time to time.

My spare bedroom was my catch-all. The CPU sat under my desk, so I used my big toe to punch the power button and scooted papers around to make room for the keyboard. With little effort, I soon connected to the world. I scanned news headlines on the opening screen and read a short story on the ongoing Middle East conflict. Nothing much had changed. *Since Cain and Abel.*

The local kennel club Web site discussed dog tags, keeping a proper fence, and tattooing your pet's ear. Tattoo identification made it easier to return a pet to its owner.

Another site brought up information on microchips like Schotzie had. But they didn't do any good until you found an animal. Not much other information was listed to prevent a snatching.

In the search box at the top of the screen, I entered *dognapping.* A long list of articles flashed up. The first story was about a family in New Hampshire who ran after two men who'd grabbed their Labrador retriever at 9:30 one morning. In broad daylight. The owner threw a pipe at the back of the vanishing Grand Am, and I wanted to cheer him. The children cried to the reporter, "Our Rocky's gone. We won't get him back." The family bred Labs and had lost puppies to thieves the season before. "The children can't even play with their own pets in our yard. Can you believe anyone would stoop so low?" The father's anger poured out on the page. I stared at the accompanying picture of two youngsters, their sad expressions so like that of John Clarence. But not Jared.

With a click, I discovered that the main purpose of dognapping was to sell the animals to research facilities. Beagles and Labradors were the most popular breeds for their purposes. My stomach roiled. Harley's number one concern had been on target.

Reading on, I gasped. You could obtain a license to sell random-source animals, ones found and not claimed, to researchers. I huffed as I read the article. "Random source, my eye!" Case after case of unscrupulous dealers, who sanctioned dognapping and made huge profits from the sales, ran a full page. A flush of anger burned my cheeks.

Another link brought me to an article about animals held for ransom. I sat up straighter, my heart rate increasing. Ransom demands? Would Ginnie receive a call about Schotzie? And how would she pay a kidnapper? With money I needed?

I read on. Preying on people who loved their dogs, kidnappers made ridiculous demands. Since the kidnappers knew where the owner lived, owners became worried about consequences if they didn't follow through and pay up.

One eighty-year-old man had his pet taken, and he used his life savings to rescue the dog. His neighbors raised funds to help him reestablish what he lost. The picture of the elderly gentleman with his arm draped around his fluffy companion made me smile. Strangers even sent money through a Web site a friend established. *There are still some good people left around, Lord.*

More articles told of others not so fortunate. I chewed my lip and pictured a frightened, lonely, older woman sitting by her telephone, cup of tea in hand, waiting to hear if her beloved doggie still lived. The thefts seemed to be rampant in Great Britain, as many as five hundred dogs stolen daily. I recalled Franklin's remark about the huge numbers of missing animals.

"Wow. That's a lot of research."

Continuing to read, I learned about puppy mills that took in younger pets and sold them to unsuspecting customers. More often than not, the puppies weren't well cared for and didn't live long or had troublesome diseases.

My eyes widened at the next link, and my stomach did flip-flops. Dog fighting enthusiasts grabbed the animals and pitted them against one another. After rigorous training and mistreatment, the precious pets were transformed into snarling beasts. I closed my eyes and pictured Seth and sweet Patches and charging dalmatians. How unfair to change an animal with such horrid abuse.

I propped my chin on my hand and visited different sites. A huge lump grew in my throat, and my eyes watered as I viewed pictures of sad-eyed dogs inside filthy cages, their coats matted, ribs protruding. Who would be so cruel? Someone looking for a fistful of dollars, that's who. I began to get nauseous over the plight of the animals.

Another search produced a few results from cities trying to quell the rising problem. Several activist groups pleaded for donations to help them demonstrate the important roles pets played in their owner's lives. I wondered how their funds were used.

A dull throb began at the back of my neck. I shut down the computer then wandered into the den and slumped on the sofa. "Lord, we live in a mean world. Even our pets aren't safe anymore." Weariness tugged me to a pillow, and I closed my eyes.

The phone's ring jerked me awake. I had dozed off and dreamed of puppies and Patches. I reached for the receiver and smiled at the greeting.

"Belle, how are you this evening?" A deep voice rumbled.

A flutter ran through my chest. "Franklin. How nice to hear from you."

"I've had you on my mind. Thought I'd give you a call and see how your day was."

Had me on his mind? Wow. I shifted to a sitting position and tugged my shirt into place. "It was busy but fine." No admission from me about my daydreams.

"Did you enjoy the dog show Saturday?"

"I did." I sighed. "I saw a clip on TV tonight about

the missing animals. Did Gordon's little girl find her dog? I thought maybe that was filmed earlier."

"No, not yet. It's such a shame."

A wave of sadness washed through me. My leg had gone to sleep, so I tapped my foot on the floor. "I just finished surfing the Web about dognapping. It's a depressing tale. And so prevalent. I never knew how many animals were stolen."

"You really have gotten interested in this, haven't you?"

"Yes." I fluffed a pillow and leaned back. "It started out personal with Ginnie and the Pampered Pooch, then the Clarence boys, but now I'm just plain mad." I started to mention Jared but still had no proof of any wrongdoing.

"What did you find out?"

I rambled on about the information I'd uncovered. "Do you suppose dog fighting takes place around here?" I shivered at the thought.

"I don't know." He paused. "Some pretty unsavory characters live all over the country, so I wouldn't be one bit surprised."

I considered his words. "Did you know our legislature is even involved in trying to keep pet theft down? A bill to amend the Animal Welfare Act and have tighter restrictions on those who sell to research facilities is in the works. I discovered that information on the Last Chance for Animals site."

Franklin coughed. "Excuse me." He fumbled with the receiver and then said, "You've really discovered good information, haven't you?"

"Yes, I have." I curled my leg under me. "Taking someone's pet is awful. I know how attached you can become to an animal. Seth and Patches were inseparable." I stopped, picturing Susanne. "When you are lonesome, a dog can fill a special spot, or so I was told by an expert." I scanned the empty room and wondered if I needed a companion. My nose wrinkled as I considered the idea.

"Seth's article about your friend's kennel was thorough. Did he mention suspects to you?"

I hesitated. "No, I haven't heard from him." Jared and Mel's names flitted through my mind.

"In light of the comment your son made, you aren't helping with an investigation, are you?"

"Me?" I gave a tinny laugh. "Why would you ask?"

"Just curious. Wouldn't want a friend to get in over her head." He blew out a breath. "This good friend, Buster, just filled my lap." Rattling sounded in my ear as Franklin and Buster got into position. "He thinks he's a puppy and jumps the minute I get comfortable."

We laughed.

"He's a Lab, right?" I kept the knowledge of the research facilities using mostly beagles and Labs to myself.

"A chocolate Lab. And Sadie's a yellow Lab." He gave a low whistle. "She's loping through the kitchen right now in search of the rest of my sandwich."

"A true garbage disposal."

He chuckled. "You've got that right. Although I try not to feed them from the table. It's healthier if they stay on their diets."

I nodded and said, "Wish I could do the same.

Maybe I need someone to monitor my eating habits after that Grady's dinner."

"You don't need to diet, Belle." A beat of silence passed. "You look just right."

"Thank you. I wasn't fishing for a compliment, but I'll take it. And the same can be said about you, Mr. Landscaper." A blush crept up my cheeks at my forwardness. Open mouth, insert foot—my specialty.

My comment was accepted with a hearty laugh. "Thanks for telling me. But I won't let it go to my head."

"So how many lawns did you cut today?" I fished for a safe subject.

He hemmed and hawed a moment. "I really didn't do any lawns." His half-hearted laugh made me smile. "I was immersed in housework. After our discussion the other night, I noticed my house needed help. Dog hair and dust coated everything."

"I thought that was my job." I bit my lip. There went the foot-and-mouth thing again.

"Well, before I can have anyone come clean my home, I have to clean it."

I giggled. "Now that makes a lot of sense. But you know, I hear that all the time. It's as though we can only show the cleaning lady so much mess, or she'll freak out."

"Are you one to freak out?"

"Oh, Franklin." I snorted. "I've lifted lizards from the laundry, scrubbed moldy bathrooms, and sifted through closets that would rival the city dump." I moaned. "I truly believe I'm becoming impervious to most messes."

"Then I'll keep that in mind," he said.

"Do that." I waited for an invitation to come clean, but he changed the subject.

"Has Seth been with the newspaper for long?"

"Yes, he's been there several years. I think he'll be a career journalist, because he surely does love his work."

"Is he an investigative reporter?"

"He covers all kinds of stories."

"I suppose he'll record what the sheriff finds about the missing dogs."

I frowned. Why was he so interested in Seth's reporting? "Uh-huh, suppose so."

"Seems to be a fine young man. I enjoyed meeting him, and Kevin has nothing but good things to say. . .about both of you."

Just a topic of conversation. Quit assuming everyone steals dogs. I squeezed my eyes shut. "That's nice to hear." The fact that I'd not been overly nice to Kevin in the last few years gave me a dose of guilt.

"Now just how is Kevin related to you?"

"He's my ex-husband's sister's boy."

"Oh." Silence ensued.

I couldn't bring myself to say more about Kevin's family. The blistering of Phoebe's tirade still hadn't faded from my mind.

"Does Seth's dad live in Jackson?" Franklin asked.

"No. Peter died in a plane crash a few years ago."

"I'm so sorry."

"Seth took it hard. He'd just begun to restore his relationship with his father." I sighed. "But the Lord knows best."

"He does. I worked hard not to question His wisdom when Kathleen died." I heard a dog bark. "Sadie's still searching for that sandwich."

I was relieved at the change of topic. Probing our former lives didn't seem timely. Did Franklin feel the same way?

We chatted another ten minutes about nothing in particular. Before he ended the conversation, Franklin said, "Belle, I'd love to have lunch with you one day."

"I'd enjoy that."

"Good. I'll be in touch. Good night." He hung up.

Disappointment welled since we hadn't set a date, and I stared at the receiver before I placed it on the charger. *Wonder if he will call. Wonder if I want him to call.* I swatted at the pillow beside me. "Get real, Belle; you sound like a teenager."

Around ten I crawled into bed and snuggled under the comforter. Franklin's warnings tickled my ears. He didn't know my vested interest in solving this crime. I pictured the window frame and Franklin on the cinder block. I shook my head. "His shoulders are too broad to fit through that window. But Jared could slither in." I turned off the lamp. I wanted to know that boy's alibi.

10

Tuesday morning, Ginnie called to claim a date for lunch. "I know you don't work until this afternoon, so why don't we have lunch? I have to get my mind and body away from this place before I go crazy."

"Sounds good. Let's try Lydia's, about twelve thirty?" I loved the small cozy tea room.

"Meet you there," Ginnie said.

Before I left to meet Ginnie, I tried Theresa's number again, but it went straight to voice mail. Aggravated, I stomped to the Jeep and grumbled all the way to lunch.

Ginnie wore a bright floral sundress and green sandals. She grabbed my elbow and stuck one foot up for me to examine. "Look at the sole. Like a tennis shoe." She released my arm. "You could wear these and update that wardrobe."

As if I could afford those, I thought. "Let's eat." I shuffled through the door in my worn-out brown sandals. "My wardrobe fits my life."

Ginnie's laugh floated upward. "For right now. We'll see if that changes."

The owner greeted us at the restaurant door. "You've done such great things with this old house." Ginnie peered at the crown molding and fresh wallpaper with tiny rosebuds. The place wasn't crowded, and Lydia seated us by a bay window.

A remodeled vintage house, each room was converted

into a unique dining area. Antique tables and mismatched sterling silver knives and forks and china gave a homey atmosphere.

"Thanks, Ginnie. It was great fun. . .although a lot of work." Lydia placed a pencil and a pad on the table. "Our special today is spinach quiche or Grandma Morales's tamales." She smiled. "A variety, no?" She toddled off, her purple Mexican dress flapping, and returned with a cut-glass pitcher of water. Filling our glasses, she said, "Ginnie, I heard about your loss at da doggie home. I'm so sorry. But I know it's not your fault. Someone means for bad, but God will turn to good. I pray."

Ginnie gave a tight smile. "Thank you, Lydia. Keep the prayers coming."

With a brisk nod, Lydia returned to the kitchen.

To place our order, we had to read the list on the pad and circle items we wanted. Each visit had a different menu. Quite a collection of dishes filled the page. Ginnie looked at a nearby patron's plate. "The food looks delicious."

I scanned the menu. "Everything I've eaten here has been wonderful." The waitress came for our orders, and we sipped peach tea while we waited for my Rosalita's chicken salad and Ginnie's special spinach quiche.

Ginnie pointed a finger at me. "No Pampered Pooch worries for this meal. Pinky promise?"

I extended my little finger and squeezed hers, hoping I could live up to it.

"So spill the beans about the new man in your life."

"I've told you all I know." I fiddled with a sweetener

packet. "He's very nice." I paused as a tiny flutter tickled my tummy. "He called last night."

Ginnie let out a squeal, and heads turned our way. "He called you?"

"Settle down. We're not in high school." I felt my cheeks flush.

"He's gotten you to blush." She squealed again. "Belle Blevins, I never thought I'd see you blush." Her eyes filled with tears.

"What's wrong?" I reached for her hand.

"I'm just so happy for you. I want you to find someone else to love." She squeezed my fingers. "Peter's deception cut you to the quick, and you've shied away from men ever since."

My eyes widened. "Ginnie, I have not."

"Name one man you visit with at church." She sat back in her chair, crossed her arms, and peered at me.

I couldn't come up with a name. "I just feel uncomfortable, that's all." The sweetener packet between my fingers tore and spilled its contents. I swiped at the mess with my napkin and looked at my friend, a sad smile tugging my lips. "I never know what to say to an available man. It's awkward."

"They've tried." She leaned forward and whispered, "I noticed Glenn Higgs flirting with you at the social last month."

"Flirting?" I smoothed my napkin in my lap. "He was just talking about his daughter's new baby."

The waitress approached with our salads and stalled our conversation. Once we'd blessed our food, I took a bite, swallowed, and pointed a fork at Ginnie.

"You know, Glenn will be showing you baby pictures before long."

Ginnie squinted. "I'm not sure I'm up to that." She wiped her mouth. "After all, I'm barely a widow."

I snorted. "Two years. Mitch has been gone two years." I tapped my tea glass with my nail. "And that, my dear, makes you eligible for Glenn's attention."

Ginnie shot me a pained look and heaved a sigh. "I'm not sure I'll ever love anyone again. Mitch was my one and only."

I nodded. "I know that. But you can't push the possibilities out of your mind." I took another bite and swallowed. "Ginnie, God may have a bigger plan for you. Look how He helped you start Pampered Pooch." I smiled. "You never thought you'd get it off the ground."

"True, but dating? Ugh." She sniffled. "God will have to flash a neon sign for that to happen." She toyed with a lettuce leaf. "Think Franklin might have a neon sign on him?"

My heart began the flutter once more. "I'm not sure, but I'm not averse to the idea. It might be fun."

Ginnie grinned. "I'm so glad to hear that. I want my best friend to have all the happiness she can get."

"Thanks, dear one. I appreciate your vote of confidence."

"So what did Franklin talk about?" She fell into her twang, "Did he speak mo' of his heritage? Is he a proper gentleman?"

I snickered. "Oh, yes, my *deah*, he's a proper gentleman." I took another bite and chewed slowly, enjoying Ginnie's anticipation.

She patted my hand. "Go on."

"We talked about the missing dogs and cleaning houses." I grinned and sipped my tea.

"Belle. You only talked dogs and business?" She shook her head. "You need some flirting lessons. If this continues, I can teach you how to bat those eyelashes and be coy."

We both let out a ring of laughter and settled in to enjoy our meal. Just as we finished, a flurry at the next table caught our attention. Violet Lester and her mother sat down. Ginnie cringed. Violet threw a look in our direction then shoved her chair from the table and approached.

"Belle, nice to see you." The monotone greeting let me know her mom had at least reared her to acknowledge others. Her gaze darted to Ginnie. "Have you had word from your insurance agent?" The tension crackled between the two women as a scowl crossed Violet's forehead. With hands on her hips, her glare bored into Ginnie's eyes.

Ginnie cleared her throat. "Not yet, Violet. I'll call as soon as I hear something."

"You just do that." She shook a red acrylic nail in Ginnie's face. "And I expect it to be soon. My Linda's sick at heart without her dog." She turned, walked back to her table, and sat, her back to us.

I leaned forward and touched Ginnie's trembling hand, our gaiety spoiled. "You okay?"

"Let's finish and leave if you don't mind." She took a sip of tea, the ice clinking in her glass as it wobbled.

Lydia brought the check when I motioned, and we left money on the table. We chose the exit farthest from Violet and her mom and headed to the porch.

"Don't let her upset you so. You can't get tangled around her axle," I said.

Ginnie stopped. "Easy for you to say. You didn't lose her very expensive dog." She took another step then wilted. "I'm sorry. It's just so upsetting." She wiped a tear from her eye. "I love animals, and the thought of something terrible happening to Schotzie. . .makes me want to lose my lunch."

I pointed to the garden alongside the walk. "Come sit down." I led the way among beautiful tulips to a bench near a tiny pond full of koi. We sat, and Ginnie's sniffles grew louder. "I know you're upset, and you have every right to be, but you didn't lose the dog. Who knew it would be stolen? It was an accident."

"One nobody seems able to fix." Her chin wobbled, and tears began to rain down her cheeks. "How can I assure a dog will be safe now? My credibility is shot." She dabbed her eyes with a tissue.

"I read an article online about being responsible pet owners." Ginnie looked up. "One suggested implanting a microchip in an animal so that if it is recovered it can be returned to the owner."

"I know about that. Schotzie has a microchip. Or at least she *had* one. But like I told Don, it's of no use unless you *find* the dog."

"Does Donetta's dog have a chip?"

Ginnie's eyes widened. "I'm not sure. Why?"

"I have an idea." I watched her face. "Why don't

you start a campaign at the kennel to help owners care for their dogs? Get her on board. She's always looking for a cause."

"A campaign?" She blew her nose, brow furrowed, and wiped mascara from under her eyes.

"Call a vet and talk to him. They have ideas for becoming responsible pet owners." I patted her hand. "You can advertise classes. I'll get the information from the Internet and print it for you." She began to brighten. "Advertise a class teaching animal care and maybe one on grooming or puppy training. Have Donetta run a raffle for the pet shelter. She'd love that exposure, and she's an expert fund-raiser after all her years in the society circles. Get the vet to speak. You know Harley would put up posters. He might even be a sponsor if he thought he could sell pet products." I thought of all the booths at the dog show.

"That might work." She chewed her thumbnail. "It would be proactive."

I nodded. "It will get you involved with the community in a positive way." I smiled. "Maybe Franklin could come speak."

Ginnie gave me a watery smile. "I could meet Mr. Wonderful and do something positive at the same time." She grasped my wrist. "Thank you for finding the diamond in the dust. I appreciate your friendship so much." She pulled me into a hug.

"Right back at you." We stood and headed toward our cars. "I'm on my way to the Johnsons' now."

"Dressed like that?" Ginnie pointed to my yellow dress and sandals.

"I have a change in the car."

"I'm on my way to get my hair trimmed." She patted her coiffure. I didn't see a stray hair that needed attention. "Lorena's the best, and I wouldn't know what to do without her."

I nodded. "She is the best. I need to call and get an appointment soon. Give her my love. And think on a date for a Saturday pet clinic."

Ginnie waved before she got into her car.

Keys in hand, I stepped into the Jeep, glad Ginnie was off to the beauty shop. Lorena's upbeat attitude would lift her spirits besides making her hair look terrific. That woman could snip any 'do into fashion.

Mulling over the vet idea, I smiled. Maybe Franklin would help Ginnie. My fingers clutched the steering wheel tighter. Asking him would give me an excuse to call. My smile spread, and the flutter began. I pressed one hand against my stomach to still the butterflies. Flipping down the visor mirror, I looked at my reflection. Maybe Lorena needed to work her magic on me soon.

Then I thought of the expense. And Ginnie's spending. New shoes, lunch, haircut. Were her cash reserves large enough for a quarterly tax payment? Anxiety gnawed away the tummy flutter.

11

It didn't take but a few minutes to circle around to my client's house. Hannah Johnson's gray brick bungalow wasn't far from Lydia's restaurant, but the neighborhood was run-down. Where the tea room's Victorian remodeling had added value to the area, this section of Trennan left a lot to be desired. I felt bad that Hannah had to settle in this dilapidated quarter of the city. I certainly wouldn't want to visit her after dark.

A single mom, Hannah worked long hours to help her son through college, so I had given her a bargain rate. We'd met in line at the grocery one day. She'd bragged to the cashier about Darren's partial scholarship to Memphis State, and we struck up a conversation since Seth had taken classes there.

Soon I began cleaning her home every other week for free. Friend to friend. Within two months, she decided to pay me. I knew the feeling associated with "free" often dragged on one's dignity, so I negotiated a low rate and accepted the checks. The two-bedroom dreary place probably just needed a touch-up this week.

I noticed an extra car in the driveway, so I parked on the street, where the curb's overgrown weeds swiped the side of my car. She sure needed my teenage yard man to work his magic. I thought of bringing over a potted plant to set by the front door on my next visit. Anything to help add some color to perk up the place.

Carrying my T-shirt, jeans, and tennis shoes, I knocked on the front door.

"Hey, Belle. Come in." Hannah packed a sandwich into a paper bag as I opened the door. "I'm running late as usual." She tucked her white blouse into her blue skirt and slid on loafers.

"No problem. I'll change and get busy. And I'll lock up when I leave."

"No, don't worry about locking the door. Darren is home." She stopped and leaned against the counter, one hand rubbing her chin, her brown eyes clouded. "Home for good, I'm afraid."

I dropped my tennis shoe and leaned over to grab it. "What happened? The semester's not over."

Tears filled her eyes, and she stepped closer to whisper, "He was caught with marijuana in his dorm room." Her mouth drooped.

I let out a gasp and caught her arm. "I'm so sorry, Hannah."

She turned and rolled down the top of the brown paper bag. "For right now, Darren's working at Greeley's store at night." She shook her head and rubbed her eyes. "I don't know what we'll do. He has a court-appointed lawyer, so I guess he'll direct our steps."

I placed my clothes on a stool. "You know, Hannah, God can direct your steps better than any lawyer."

Hannah's grim look silenced me. "I know you mean well, Belle, but look at what happened to you." She shook her head. "I don't think I want any part of a God who lets people down all the time, especially people like you."

"Whoa, wait a minute." I extended my hand, palm up. "God didn't let me down. My ex made his own choices." I leaned toward her. "God's walked beside me every step of the way. No, He didn't let me down at all."

She closed her eyes for a brief moment and then picked up the sack. "Thanks for all you do."

My heart filled with heaviness. "I'll pray."

She gave a small smile and left me in the kitchen. I heard her car start and the tires squeal as she backed into the street. Much to my dismay, the months of witnessing to my new friend hadn't taken root. The invitation to church had been flatly turned down. But that didn't mean I couldn't invite her again.

No sooner had she gone than Darren entered the room. He was slight in build with large, dark eyes and thick, brown hair. Today he lacked his usual personal hygiene. He smelled.

"Darren. Nice to see you."

He glared at me, pulled a soda from the refrigerator, and made a hasty retreat down the hall. I wondered why a handsome, smart fellow would make such stupid choices in life. But then my handsome, smart husband fell in the same category.

"Lord, this household needs more cleaning than I can provide. It needs the Holy Spirit." With a shake of my head, I carried my clothes to the bathroom and changed.

The next hour was spent tidying up. I approached Darren's room and saw that he was on the computer.

I'd leave it until last if I even worked in there at all.

As I cleaned the living room, the vacuum shut off. I flipped the switch then turned to look at the plug. Darren held it in one hand.

He flapped the cord back and forth. "I couldn't talk to you over the noise." I stared at him. His countenance had hardened, and he appeared angry. I wondered if drugs ran through his system.

I lifted an eyebrow, feigning bravado. "Did you need something?"

"I'm going out for a while." He bent over and plugged in the vacuum, and noise filled the room as he strode out. I watched him leave, my anger flaring under the surface over his rude behavior.

"Lord, please make Your presence known to Hannah and Darren," I prayed with each vacuum swipe across the floor. It seemed the bright young man I once knew had evaporated.

Darren's bedroom door stood ajar as I approached, vacuum in hand. I pushed it with one foot to get in. Darkness shrouded the room, the computer screen saver flickering brightly. I flipped on the overhead light and gathered candy wrappers and soda cans from the desk. More junk food containers filled the wastebasket. With his build, this diet would pudge him up in a hurry. I paused, a sticky wrapper between my fingers. I'd heard smoking marijuana caused the munchies. I sniffed the air then chuckled. Like I'd be able to detect one odor from another in this smelly dungeon.

Tossing the comforter on top of the bed, I kneeled and scooped out trash from underneath. Darren was a pig. I reached for something wedged under the headboard. It was a small plastic baggie. My fingers jerked away as I realized what it might contain. This would have to be Hannah's decision. I would call her later, but I wasn't fooling around with drugs. As a matter of fact, if Darren continued to stay, this might be my last visit. I stood, smoothed the sheets, and plumped the pillow. Resisting the urge to check the baggie, I tugged the comforter into place.

Suddenly the room plunged into darkness. I whirled about expecting to see Darren at the door. No one was there. My heart slowed to its regular rhythm. I flipped the switch—the lightbulb had burned out. With a sigh, I stepped toward his desk to turn on a lamp and bumped the computer mouse.

MySpace.com filled the screen. I remembered Mark's Web site page. This held Darren's profile listing. I leaned in and read some of his entry, his favorite music and food, movies he'd seen. He'd fudged about his age; he certainly was not twenty-four. Self-employed? I knew better than that. Sign: Libra. Orientation? Oh, single and straight. I shuddered. The world had sure changed. Studying the picture he posted, I noticed the distant, almost vacant look in his eyes. I slid the mouse beside the keyboard. Evil was present here. I made haste to finish my work, praying each minute.

Once I stepped into the garage with the trash, curiosity nibbled. What else did this mysterious boy have listed on his computer site? I chewed on my lip, replaced the garbage can lid, and wandered into the kitchen. I swept the floor and ruminated. Should

Hannah know about her son's doings online? If I were going to talk to her about his drug stash, maybe I could discover other things on his Web site. I poured myself a glass of water and created a mental checklist of good reasons to return to the computer. Self-employed—what did he mean? Dealing drugs?

With my last swallow, I chuckled. *Yeah, Belle, rationalize your plain old curiosity. That's all it is, you know.* With a frown, I gave in. I wasn't exactly sure how to navigate the Web and find his information from my home computer, so I'd just do it now.

I peeked out the front window and saw Darren's car was still gone. Returning to the bedroom, I pulled out the desk chair and tapped the mouse. His face filled the screen once again.

I scrolled down the page and gaped at the pictures posted. Certainly not like Mark's site. Evidently the friends Darren had listed didn't mind baring their souls, much less their bodies. Crude remarks and captions brought a blush to my cheeks. Suggestive poses left little to the imagination. Some of the remarks, especially those made by girls, would blister the paint from the wall.

Darren hadn't only lied about his age. His occupation certainly wasn't self-employed. And he believed in inner-dimensional travel? This young man was in a world of his own! A song played as I skipped through the pictures. The cold lyrics were hard to understand, but I knew most rap music left much to be desired.

Returning to his home page, I peered at Darren's

face. His brown eyes bored into my heart. I threw out prayers for his salvation and safety and then slid the chair away from the desk. I hadn't found any incriminating evidence, so I'd have little to report. I left, my heart shrouded with a heavy cloak. Hannah surely did have her work cut out, and she didn't believe in the power of prayer. Only Jesus could dispel the evil and darkness I'd just witnessed. How did people manage without God in their lives?

During my last sweep of the kitchen, I gathered my clothes and wondered about telling Hannah. She didn't have a cell phone, and I wanted her to know what was going on soon. I found a piece of paper and scribbled a note for her to call me and then walked to her bedroom and tucked it under her pillow. Pushing the lock button, I hoped Darren had kept a house key. If he hadn't, his attitude toward me would certainly not improve.

The cloud of gloom accompanied me to my car. I cranked on the motor and turned the radio to a Christian station. I needed praise music in the worst way. I sang along with the first song then realized I could use fellowship, too. Running my fingers through my hair, I thought of Ginnie's beauty shop appointment.

I tumbled some calculations through my brain and decided I could afford a haircut. Yes, a visit to the Cactus Flower would do me a lot of good.

I turned on Braun Road. Joining in another song, I began to relax. I slowed for a school zone and a line of SUVs picking up children. Just then a cat dashed across the road, a brown dog in hot pursuit. I slammed on my brakes, heart racing, and watched them career around a corner.

Animals missing from their yards. Maybe these would return. Would Schotzie? I bit my lip. I still hadn't reached Theresa. I looked in the rearview mirror and cringed. Traffic was backed up. Mechanically, I continued my drive, my thoughts running the list of suspects. I'd leave out Franklin. But would Darren fit through that window?

12

I rang Lorena's salon and found she had an opening.

"Belle, how are you? It's been a coon's age since you've been by. Or so it seems." Her cheery greeting and peck on the cheek lifted my spirits immediately.

Christian praise music filled the air, and the sweet scent of shampoo tickled my nose. The terra-cotta walls and cream silk window shades were soothing to the eye.

"Pour yourself a glass of cranberry water"—she motioned, comb in hand, toward the corner of the shop—"and I'll be with you in just a second."

A carafe and ice bucket sat on a wrought-iron table beside a stack of magazines. I lifted a heavy crystal glass and filled it. With the first sip, tension seeped from my shoulders in the pleasant atmosphere. Her shop was a haven for relaxation. I knew we would spend the next hour relating events about our friends and family. But I didn't plan on talking about lost dogs.

She rang up her previous customer's charges and turned to me. "Come on back here, girl. We've got some catching up to do."

I followed her to the shampoo sinks. As she scrubbed my scalp, I asked about her dad, who had Alzheimer's. "He's doing well. My sister found a new assisted living home, and he's adapting wonderfully." She pulled a towel from the cabinet and draped it over my head. Returning to her station, she said, "I don't know, Belle. I live day to day, asking Jesus to care for him and keep me from getting that dreadful disease." She swung the chair around for me to sit.

I towel dried my hair. "I know the feeling." And I did know, having nursed my mother through the illness to her death after Peter left. "We can only put our trust and thought life in His hands and leave the future up to Him."

"That's so right." She pulled a rolling cart next to her and looked at my reflection in the mirror, her eyes twinkling. "I just want to tell you how glad I am you're my friend." She shook a black barber's cape and slid it around my shoulders, her petite frame stretching to make it flow over my head. Her tiny feet were in colorful espadrilles, and she wore a cute denim outfit. Even though Lorena worked long hours, she never looked weary or unkempt. She greeted every customer with a cheery attitude as though she was the only one she'd expected all day.

"Because you're a good one. Ginnie told me about the dog being stolen and how you stood right by her side when she confronted Violet." Lorena's mouth pulled down. "Bless her heart; like Ginnie needed that worry."

"It's been hard on her." *And me.*

"Theresa Clarence was in here yesterday. She said Don was investigating their missing dogs as well." She gripped my shoulders and whispered, "He even questioned her boys. Can you imagine? Those little kids?"

Actually I could, but I kept my thoughts to myself.

"Theresa was as nervous as a long-tailed cat in a room full of rocking chairs." She chuckled. "But let's allow the sheriff's department to worry, because right now I want some good news. Got any?"

"I do have a little news." I shook off images of Jared and gave a soft laugh. "And its part of the reason I wanted to get spruced up."

"Tell me." She looked in the mirror again, her eyes twinkling. "What's he like?"

I stuck out my lip in a pout. "Did Ginnie already break the story?"

"She did, and I've been waiting fifteen minutes for you to bring it up." She laughed and put her hands on my shoulders. "Ginnie said you'd been seen in the company of a very nice-looking man, and then she dug through my stack of papers until she found a picture of the two of you." She spun the chair and began to snip. "Is he Mr. Right?"

"I have no idea. He's Mr. Right Now, though." I gave a nervous laugh.

"Belle, I've never seen you so girly before." Lorena paused, comb in the air. "I think spring fever has caught you, or you are in love."

"What did you feel like when you met your sweetie?" Her first husband had passed away, and she was now married to a good-looking, tall Texan.

She gazed across the room with a faraway look in her eyes for a moment and then turned to me. "I just knew. He swept me off my feet." She put her hands on her hips, shaking her head. "I'd been looking in the wrong places for years, and suddenly God brought him into my life at church. He came to visit his mama and took her to Sunday services. Who could turn down a guy like that?" The scissors began to sing again. "Is this guy a Christian?"

"He is." I related the prayer he'd prayed for Susanne and her lost dog. "It was so special."

"Well, I'm happy for you." She swung the chair to face the mirror. "And whatever we can do to make you look gorgeous to catch his eye, we will do. You wanna go red?" We laughed at the standard joke.

"No, remember?" I lifted a strand of hair. "I worked hard to get every one of these gray hairs, and I'm keeping 'em. They are badges of honor." I fingered my bangs. *Yes, I'm earning more, too, worrying about missing pooches.*

Lorena's eyes gleamed. "Then let's get them spruced up." She eyed me in the mirror and then said, "I tell you what, let's wax and color your eyebrows. Add some color to your face." She slid a box from the cabinet below the mirror. "This is a vegetable dye I've been using. Reduces any allergic reactions." Her lips tipped up. "What do you think?"

I looked at my pale reflection, grinned, and nodded.

By the time she wove her magic, I felt beautiful. That was the perk of being Lorena's client. She always made your appointment special. I paid her and left, walking on air, Franklin on my mind. My dark mood and growing suspicions had definitely been dispelled.

When I got home, I spent some time in the yard. It had cooled by evening, and I watered the flowers and swept the porch and driveway. Belinda and Mel greeted me as they left to go to dinner.

It was too awkward to ignore them, so I hollered, "Y'all heading to Grady's?"

"Ha. I wish," Mel said with a groan. "They don't serve rabbit food there."

Belinda poked him in the side. "I want him to live a long time, so I'm taking care of him. Yet he complains." She grasped his arm. "Poor dear, he's so mistreated."

Mel held a small packet in the air. "Got me chewing gum so I won't feel hungry. It ain't workin' so good."

The packet didn't look like it contained bubblegum. I watched as they climbed into Mel's truck. He wasn't the best-looking guy in the world, yet the gorgeous, dark-haired, petite woman acted as though she adored him. And he seemed so unhappy lately, bitter. I recalled his flirting with Ginnie and Violet's remark about his reputation. No sign of marriage strains tonight. He wouldn't be mad enough to try to harm her business. Surely not. I chewed on my lip. He could fit through that window though. But then so could Jared and Darren. He was chewing gum. "Good grief, are all the gum-chewing folks in Trennan going on my list?"

I took one more swipe with the broom and collapsed in a porch chair. Tiny fireflies lit the evening. A soft breeze cooled my brow and brushed in lovely sweet smells from the flowers. A lone star peeked and flickered in the twilight. I lifted my face and recited the old rhyme: "I wish I may, I wish I might. . ." I stopped. "I wish. . ." Yet I couldn't for the life of me fill in the blank.

I closed my eyes.

Lord, I wish for what You have for me. You say You

will give us the desires of our hearts, but I don't even know
what those desires are. I guess You'll have to surprise me.

I opened my eyes and smiled. I was sure that star
winked at me.

I rocked in an effort to unwind completely. But
with the back-and-forth cadence, my worries drew to
the surface and my fingers rapped a beat on the chair's
arm. My household account couldn't sustain me and
pay property taxes. I did have a small savings account.
If I added money from. . .

"Man. I'll drive myself crazy if I don't stop. Between
money and suspects, my mind's in a frenzy."

It had grown dark, and hunger drove me to the
kitchen where I pulled out a frozen dinner and nuked
it. The aroma of chicken spaghetti filled the house. I
made some tea, filled a plate, and sat down to read the
paper. Nothing was mentioned about the dognappings.
I hit the TV remote and skimmed some channels, but
nothing worth watching appeared, so I turned it off.
Returning my dishes to the kitchen, Darren flickered
through my mind, and I had an urge to use the
computer.

I booted it up and googled MySpace. In a few
seconds the main page appeared. I read through the fine
print and discovered that to access people's sites, you
needed your own account. I chewed my lip. I didn't want
to use my real name, so I came up with Miss Feather.
That was close enough.

I didn't fill out the profile page completely or
accurately, but in just a few seconds, I had a "friend"
connect to my site. I wasn't sure what to do next, so I

ignored the provocative picture.

"What if I croak and my son comes in to check my computer?" Here would be all this sexy stuff on the monitor! "Can't have that."

At the top of the screen was a search box. I typed in Darren Johnson's name and quite a number of links appeared. I scrolled down the page until I saw his picture. One click drew me to his page. Again I scrolled down and saw some more photos of his groupies. A blog area was listed. I knew many people kept this online journal called a blog, but to enter his, I had to subscribe. At this point, I knew I didn't want to do that.

Curious, I tried to think of other teenagers I knew. I typed in Jared Clarence. He had no hits. Then I entered John Clarence. He had an account. It wasn't anything like Darren's, but more innocent like Mark's. John's picture with the dalmatians was so funny. He talked about his love for his pets and how he took care of them. Some comments were made from others, one called Pet Lovers. Again I hesitated to click any open.

Linda Lester had an account, Schotzie center stage. There were several photos of Linda and the prize-winning animal. She had a list of her championship points and a link to the site about their breeding business. I opened it. The Lester Show Dogs. What would happen to Linda's college fund if Schotzie wasn't returned? My stomach clenched. They'd lose a ton of money off that one dog. I didn't realize what big business they did have for Schotzie and some other schnauzers. I understood Ginnie's hysteria a little more. The professional pictures on their Web site left one with the impression of a knowledgeable breeder and handler. At least I was impressed.

Another teen crossed my mind—Ginnie's helper, Charlie Baker. I typed in his name, and sure enough, there was his picture. His leg was thrown over a ten-speed, hair spiked in a trendy fashion. He looked quite handsome. I read his profile where he fudged about being a manager at the food chain. He also mentioned a partnership in a kennel. He expounded about the Pampered Pooch and what it had to offer patrons. There was an interior shot of Schotzie sitting on her velveteen sofa. I laughed. Ginnie would be pleased at the free advertisement.

Charlie discussed his duties, blowing them out of proportion a bit to give that sense of self-importance. Being responsible for opening and closing the kennel? I wasn't so sure that could be true. But in this new world of cyberspace where no one knew quite what to believe, I supposed no harm could be done with a tad of embellishment. Hadn't I just fudged on my own account? I stared at Charlie's picture. The cocky grin plastered on his face jolted me. Charlie. He'd be able to cross that windowsill. And he'd know Schotzie's worth, having been around Violet and Linda at the kennel. My eyes narrowed. Charlie. A definite suspect to add to the list.

Before shutting down the computer, I googled my son's name and discovered he did not have a MySpace account but did have several articles linked to his name. I opened the latest and skimmed information about the Jackson city council meeting. A boring topic, Seth had at least interjected a tad of humor.

On a whim, I typed in Lauren Cooper's name. Lo and behold, a Web site popped up for her dog-breeding business. A lovely picture of Lauren surrounded by three Chihuahuas made me smile. As I read the text, no mention was made of a husband or a child. Only her "children," the dogs. My mind raced to the dog show. She had probably been there, and we hadn't seen her. Or I hadn't seen her. I wondered if Seth crossed her path.

Maybe I'll ask around. She was sure a sweetie, and Seth showed such interest at one time. Couldn't hurt. Or could it? I ran a hand over my eyes. *Tootsie Roll, Belle.*

One evening Seth had grown aggravated with my questions about his personal life. He had a king-sized Tootsie Roll in his hand at the time. He tossed it on the floor and pointed to it.

"This is a boundary." He jumped over it. "This is Belle Blevins jumping over said boundary." He frowned. "Get it, Mother? Stop jumping over the Tootsie Roll." He left the room, but the concrete example stuck. From then on, all it took was a lifted hand and the words "Tootsie Roll" to make me quit probing.

I frowned and chewed my lip. Looking up Lauren for Seth would probably constitute a Tootsie Roll.

Growing sleepy, I was losing interest in my search. Suddenly another name popped into my brain. Franklin Jeffries. His Web site dealt with landscaping and all the facets of his business. He ran three trucks and had quite a staff.

I stared at his picture on the screen. Fine lines spread from his twinkling, coffee-with-cream eyes, and a smile lit his tan face, showing off dimples. A few strands of silver hair were out of place. I traced his straight nose and strong chin with one finger. He had on a plaid shirt, the lumberjack outdoor look. My heart raced. I could get used to that face in a hurry.

Before my daydreams took on a life of their own, I turned off the computer to get ready for bed. I stared at my reflection as I brushed my teeth and felt a blush rise when I recalled Franklin's smile. He was one fine-looking man.

The phone trilled. Rushing from the bathroom to catch it, I tripped over a tennis shoe, banged my shin against the vanity stool, and bent my right big toe in an unusual direction. I clutched my leg and hop-skipped to answer, rubbing sore spots and gritting my teeth from the pain. I knew I'd be black and blue before morning.

"Hello?" I answered irritably.

"Belle, what's wrong?" Concern in Franklin's voice washed over me.

I rubbed my toe and glared at the errant shoe. "I just tripped. I'm fine." If I was this housekeeper extraordinaire, why couldn't my own home be tidy?

Franklin paused. "I'm glad to know that, although you sound like you've been in a race and lost." He laughed a hollow laugh. "I hope my call didn't cause you to be injured."

"No, no, I'm really okay." The blue welt had already begun, and my toe throbbed, but Franklin's voice diverted my thoughts. "What's going on in your world?"

"Actually I wanted to know if you'd like to go flea market shopping on Saturday."

"Flea market? Don't know that I need any fleas at the moment." I forced a little laugh.

Franklin said, "I don't either. Buster and Sadie drag in enough for me. But I know you've been interested in this dognapping business, and today on a job site I heard some talk about dogs for sale at the flea market."

A funny grunt and a gasp sounded in my ear. A sheet of paper rattled near the phone. "Sorry, lost the directions."

I stifled a giggle. Despite his workouts, he still groaned, too. Age didn't just affect me. Comforting thought.

He continued, "It's out on the highway toward Reelfoot Lake. I have no idea if we'd learn anything, but I thought it would be worth the time. What do you think?"

"You know, Harley at the pet store mentioned dogs were sold in flea markets." I scratched my head. "I'd really be interested in going."

"Well, we could just ask around then pass on any information to Kevin. I don't want to get involved with shady characters, but we could certainly do some footwork."

"Footwork." I glanced at my swollen toe. "That's what I do best. Count me in."

"Super. I'll pick you up around eight."

"I'll be ready." We said our good nights, and I hobbled to bed nursing my sore leg.

The flea market. I'd definitely keep my eyes peeled for dognappers. As I crawled under the sheet and pulled up the comforter, I smiled. I'd see those gorgeous eyes soon.

Early Saturday, I sat on the porch tapping my toes. Nervous anticipation made it hard to sleep, my dreams filled with a certain landscaper. My morning makeup routine lengthened; even with a shaky hand, my eyeliner was straight. I'd chosen a hot pink shirt and gray slacks but kept my sore toe in tennis shoes for a day of walking.

I sat in a rocker, sipping my diet drink and waiting. Morning dew misted the grass in a sprinkle of diamonds. Birds sang a greeting to the day. In the distance I could hear a lawn mower whir as someone got a start before heat set in. I knew Mel would join the yard work scene as soon as he could, and I hoped I could duck out before he appeared. I had no wish to hear his complaints today.

Peter had never been one for working outside alone. He wanted me by his side. And with Seth, it had been hard to make the time, so we'd never made yard-of-the-month. I grinned as I realized how unimportant that title had been. I'd never wanted the first place sign the neighborhood association awarded stuck in my flower bed. And in my new home, my only objective was to keep from embarrassing my neighbors, certainly not to impress them.

Franklin's pickup truck came into view, and my heart fluttered. I pushed against my chest with one hand—this frequent Franklin-caused sensation set up an erratic pulse and a flushed face. I needed time to examine these renewed feelings. I surely wasn't going to set myself up for another fall. I tucked the thought in my junk drawer for another day.

I stepped inside to grab my purse and dump my soda. By the time he'd pulled in the driveway, I stood on the steps ready to go.

"Good morning." He swung down from the truck and walked around to open my door. He swatted dog hair from the truck seat then held my arm and helped me clamber in.

I'd forgotten how nice it was to be treated like a lady. The flutter again. I stifled a cough within the musty truck cab since the inside hadn't seen a vacuum in quite a while. Some things you just politely overlook.

As I reached for the seat belt, Franklin's grip on my elbow loosened. "Looks like we'll have a pretty nice day to look for fleas."

I laughed. "If that's all we need to do, just walk through the grass in my backyard. I'm sure you'll find all you can use there."

He chuckled. "No telling what treasures we'll find. As they say, one man's junk is—"

"Another's treasure. Yeah, that might be true. I'd love to unearth a rare find." I buckled my seat belt. "But I'm not antique savvy, so I'm afraid his junk might become mine." *Unless it's a purebred schnauzer.*

He slid in the driver's seat, and his eyes ranged up and down my face. My ears heated up. "You look mighty fresh this morning."

The heat crept into my cheeks. "Thank you." If I

kept my answers short, maybe I'd keep my foot out of my mouth.

Franklin turned the key and began to back up. "Your yard could use some upkeep." He wheeled into the street. "Maybe we can barter services—landscaping and cleaning."

"Now there's a thought." Short answer. I noted the grime and dog hair on the dashboard and wondered at the state of his den.

He shifted into drive. "A pretty good one, if I do say so myself." He winked.

I thought the veins in my forehead would burst. How much blushing could a face handle at my age?

Franklin took a winding country road lined with kudzu-covered trees and a few budding dogwoods. Jonquils and buttercups swayed in the slight breeze. A purple hue covered the grass where wild hyacinth grew. Soon the rhododendron and azaleas would sprinkle in their colors. Spring in full force. Sun filled my soul.

We kept the windows rolled down, and the fresh, sweet air blew out doggy odor. An earthen smell filled the cab of the truck. I watched fields flicker by, tilled, ready for planting.

Franklin broke the silence. "Did your family farm in this area?"

I nodded, my hand out the window playing with the air current, riding up and down. "Daddy had about twenty-five acres next to his older brother. We had a big garden and grew some cotton." My lips tightened. "My brothers and I had to pick on occasion, and that was no fun. I hated it." A shudder tickled my spine.

"Mostly because I was scared of what I'd find when I reached for a cotton boll. Eww, weevils."

Franklin laughed. "Still have the farm?"

"Not all of it. Sold some to my uncle after the folks died and leased the rest. Daddy took the sheriff's job when I was eleven, and he pretty much let my uncle run all the fields." I leaned back against the headrest, the cool breeze fanning my face, memories warming my heart. "Daddy loved law enforcement more than he did farming, although Mama wasn't keen on the idea." I could picture him in his khaki uniform, a badge over his pocket, gun belt slung low. I'd never felt a moment of fear when I stood next to my dad.

"Don't think I knew he'd been the sheriff." He looked my way. "Didn't Seth want to be a policeman or fireman when he was growing up? Most boys do."

I grinned. "No, Seth wanted to be president."

Franklin laughed. "Seriously?"

"Seriously." I scrunched up my eyes and could picture my little boy's earnest face at the breakfast table.

"Mommy, when I'm big, I'm going to be the president of our country." He'd made his announcement in third grade. "I know how to do the job. You read a lot of stuff and get smart like me." Pouring milk into his cereal, he said, "You get to be 'portant and tell others what to do." He took a huge bite. Milk dribbled from his chin, and he swiped at it with his sleeve. "I'd like that, I think."

I chuckled at the memory. "As his mom, I was sure he'd make a great president."

"No bias there, eh?" He swung around a corner. "What did his dad have to say?"

I frowned at the mention of Peter. "He told him to pray about his decision."

"Always good advice."

"Yes, it was." I stared at the rolling landscape. "Peter was full of good advice."

Franklin tapped the steering wheel with his college ring. "Belle, Kevin told me a little about your divorce the other day. I rode with him to pick up Mosey. . . ." He glanced at me. "Well, I asked him. He didn't volunteer information." He tapped the wheel again. "I'm sorry, you've been through a great deal."

I slid up some in the seat, one tennis-shoe-clad foot on the dashboard, bracing for the curves ahead. My stomach clenched, and I chewed my lip before I spoke.

"I wrestled with God a good bit after Peter left, asking why and wondering what I'd done wrong. I finally concluded that asking why didn't make a difference in my life, but knowing Jesus did." I faced him, a knee in the seat. "So that's what I have tried to do. Know Jesus better. Shifting my focus to Him kept me from becoming a bitter old woman, I think." I toyed with a thread on my shirt's hem. *I admit, Lord, lately I've not been as focused.*

"Old? You certainly aren't old. And from what I can see, you aren't bitter, either. So your plan must be working." He extended a hand and touched my knee, setting off the heart flutter. "I'm glad, too. Bitterness would only eat you up—it never harms the other person."

"Don't I know that?" I shrugged. "I had an aunt who was so bitter against her ex-husband she took all the family photos and poked his eyes out with a pin."

Franklin snorted. "Now that's a bitter woman."

"Sad to say, she stayed that way till she passed out of this life." I shook my head, recalling Aunt Myna's actions. "I determined early on, after Peter left, that I wasn't walking that path. Wouldn't be good for Seth."

"I agree." He pressed the brake as we drew up behind a tractor. "Are your brothers still in the area?" He lifted an eyebrow.

I smiled. "No, those buzzards flew the coop as soon as they could." I peered out the window, a heart tug filling my eyes with tears. "I don't see them often enough." I closed my eyes against the breeze. "Lloyd is in Houston, and Marcus headed to California. He moves around." I pictured my brawny brothers in their high school rodeo days. All the girls were after the good-looking Clark boys. Mel's face flitted through my brain. He'd been a ladies' man on the rodeo grounds. I'd forgotten about his pick-up lines he used on barrel-racing girls in their tight jeans. He must be back to his old ways if he was flirting with Ginnie. Who else was on his radar?

We made a right turn off the highway and followed a line of cars. "Looks like we're getting closer to the sale." I took a tissue from my purse and dabbed at my nose.

Franklin said, "Belle, one last thing"—he gave a small smile—"it was Peter's loss."

A tingle ran through me at his softly spoken words.

"Thanks," I whispered and ducked my head. *What a kind man, this Franklin.*

A beefy attendant stood at the gate of a cleared field and took five dollars for parking; then his partner directed us to an available space. Franklin maneuvered the truck through a small ditch and around stubble and then stopped. We stepped out and did our best to avoid cow patties all the way to an asphalt court where booths and tables were set up.

I grinned at Franklin. "Where are the fleas?"

"Probably just about anywhere." He stomped dirt clods from his boots and scanned the area. "And for sure, under my truck. Where do you want to start?"

"It's so pretty today, let's just wander. I want to see everything." The warmth of the sunshine on my arms and neck felt good. It would soon soar to the nineties though, so we needed to get a move on in the cool of the morning.

"Your wish, ma'am." He touched my elbow, and we began to stroll.

All sorts of handcrafted items were on display. Reelfoot Lake's cypress tree products held center stage. Cypress-knobbed lamps and cypress-hewn boxes were everywhere. The pungent smell filled the air.

"You know the legend of Reelfoot Lake?" I asked Franklin.

He shook his head. "Don't believe I do."

I grabbed my face in feigned horror. "Then I must fill you in. We can't be this close to Reelfoot and you not know the true story."

"You're so right." He sauntered down the first row.

"Tell me all while we look for dog cages."

"Well, it's said in the early 1800s the Chickasaws were ruled by a mighty chief who had a son born with a clubfoot. The child's name translated to Reelfoot because of his unsteady gait. The young man grew up and became the chief. He wanted a wife, so he traveled south, where he found a beautiful Choctaw princess. But the girl's father didn't want her to marry a deformed man."

Franklin tsked-tsked. "So politically incorrect."

I continued, "The Choctaw chief spoke to the great spirits, who told young Reelfoot that if he took the princess, they would show their wrath upon his land. They'd cause the rocks to sway and the waters to swallow his whole village." I whispered, "And he disobeyed."

Franklin bent closer. "What happened?"

"He stole Laughing Eyes for his bride and carried her here. During the marriage ceremony, the rocks began to rumble and the earth began to tumble." I crushed my tennis shoe onto the ground, pain gripping my toe. "And with one stomp and a swoosh of water, the lake was formed."

"Whoa. Guess I never heard that version." Franklin spun and approached the second row, walking backward, a gleam in his eye. "Mine was more scientific. Had to do with earthquakes in the early 1800s. Some of the strongest on record. One version said the quake caused people in Washington, D.C., to awaken." He patted my shoulder. "Not nearly as colorful a story as yours."

I giggled. "If something caused people in D.C. to wake up, that would be a miracle in itself."

Franklin chuckled at my joke and linked elbows. "Let's go look for some flea-bitten dogs."

Beaded necklaces, hand-painted shirts, and a scrapbook area were the first booths.

Local jams and jellies filled cardboard tables in a 4-H club booth. "We're fund-raising," a pimply-faced teenager said. "It's to raise money to send our officers to a regional meeting." Franklin fished out a five-dollar bill and toted a sack of jelly.

Pies to pickles lined the row ahead of us. "Think we need to sample anything over there?" He nodded at the bread table, the aroma making my mouth water.

"Maybe on our way out." I sniffed the air. *Step away from the bread, Belle.*

Hand-tied fishing lures dangling from a stretched clothesline caught my attention as they twisted and turned in the breeze. "I wish I'd brought more cash. I could've stashed away some Christmas presents. Those would be great for Seth."

Franklin patted his back pocket. "I can make you a loan."

I flapped my hand. "Oh no, I really don't need to buy things now. They'd join the other hidden gifts I haven't found from last year. Early shopping is really pointless for me."

"Belle." Mock horror crossed his face. "I thought you were Miss Organization."

"*Moi?* Not so, my friend." I laughed. "I can clean and take care of other people, but when it comes to

Belle Blevins, look out." I stumbled on a rough piece of pavement, and Franklin grabbed my hand. "See what I mean? Look out."

Franklin grinned and continued to hold my hand as we walked.

On the last row, a lone battered pickup truck was attached to a horse trailer. The bed of the truck held several animal cages. Franklin nodded in their direction and squeezed my fingers. My pulse picked up. I checked my gait, quelling the urge to run and see. Instead we slowly meandered that way.

"Mornin' ma'am," a gap-toothed man with greasy black hair and a big belly spoke as I approached. He hitched his overalls and grinned. "Looking for a pet? I've got some mighty fine ones." He spit a tobacco stream over his shoulder as a cacophony of barks and whines filled the air.

"Aw, dear." I winked at Franklin and clutched his arm. "Look at the puppies." I stuck one finger inside a cage to stroke a small bundle of fur. "What kind is this one?" The stench from the cages assaulted my nose.

The seller took a look and said, "Poodle." He slid a sheet of paper from a folder tucked under his arm. "She's got good bloodlines, too."

I looked at the diagram. It listed the dog's ancestral line and had AKC written across the top. "Oh, she's pedigreed?"

"Yes, ma'am." His eyebrows knitted. "She's got papers."

I noted he didn't say what kind of papers. "Well how much does she cost?"

"Seven hundred fifty." He rolled his eyes. "A bargain."

My eyes grew wide. "That's a lot of money for a tiny pooch."

The man frowned. "No, ma'am. Not for an AKC dog. I wouldn't be selling my stock this cheap, but I got a bad heart and have to quit the business." He patted his chest and coughed.

"Wouldn't it be better to take them to a pet store? I know of one not far from here." I smiled.

"You know, I'd rather give a person a bargain. You can name your own price at a flea market." He winked. "We might be able to bargain on this here pup."

I released Franklin's arm. "Well thank you, but I don't think we would want a poodle anyway."

"No, dear." Franklin's eyes twinkled. "Not another Fifi in our house, please." He scanned the other animal-filled cages.

The man rubbed his whiskered chin. "What kind of dog did you have in mind?"

"No particular. . ." Franklin began.

"A schnauzer is what I'd really like. Not a puppy though." I laughed and waved my hand. "I've spent my life cleaning up messes." I leaned in closer, trying not to gag over the smell of his breath. "What I want is a little older dog, maybe even a year old. And I love schnauzers. My grandparents were German." I batted my eyelashes.

Franklin gripped my arm and spoke in clipped words, "Dear, I don't see a schnauzer in the bunch. I guess we need to look elsewhere." He tugged at me gently. "Let's shop some more. Christmas, you know."

"Hard to come by, them kind." I nodded and began to step away when the seller spoke, "Might have one for you."

I turned. "Really?"

Franklin shook his head. "No, we're not interested right now. Thanks though." He guided me away from the truck and back into the milling crowd. "Belle, what was that about?"

"Schotzie." I folded my arms across my chest. "If he had stolen dogs, maybe he had Schotzie, and I could get her back for Ginnie." *And she won't lose her reputation and my property taxes can be paid.*

"I didn't bring you here to inquire about specific dogs." A tad of irritation tinged his voice. "These guys are unsavory. Did you see him?" He huffed and bunched his fist, the jelly bag flapping against his leg. "And those dogs were in bad condition." He hung one thumb in his pocket. "This wasn't a good idea after all." He frowned. "I should've just told Kevin what I'd heard and let his men check out the lead."

I cast a glance over my shoulder and saw another couple with the poodle. "It's just sickening to think that he'll profit from those poor dogs." I started to gnaw at my thumbnail then realized how dirty my fingers were. I jerked my hand from my mouth and stuck it in my pocket.

Franklin began to walk away. "Well, little we can do now. We'll just report this to Kevin. I did get the man's license plate number, just in case."

"That's good," I murmured. How could I get back

around to check those dog pens? My eyes widened as I saw a lady reach in and pick up the poodle. The tobacco spewing man would be busy with her. "Franklin, I'm thirsty. Wasn't there a lemonade stand over one row?"

He nodded. "Let's go get some."

"Actually, would you go?" I hesitated. "I want to barter for some pickles with the lady in the middle. I'll meet you back here." I smiled up at him Ginnie-fashion.

His puzzled look gave me a moment of anxiety. Then he said, "Okay, I'll just be a minute."

When he turned, I stopped by a pickle stand and purchased a jar of dill pickles I didn't need. Then I wheeled around and jogged back the way we came. Circling next to the trailer, I peered through the slats at a pile of empty crates. No dogs. I slid beside the truck's bed, bent at the knees so I'd not be spotted. Of course I didn't account for the noise the starving, lonely pooches would stir up. Yipping and yapping, they gave me away. I straightened, opened my purse, and pulled out my address book. Tearing out a blank page, I scribbled my first name only and my telephone number. I stood on tiptoe and saw Franklin's back as he wove through the crowd toward the lemonade stand. Taking a deep breath, I headed toward the front of the puppy truck.

The lady cuddled the poodle and spoke lovingly in baby talk. The gap-toothed man grinned. He looked up as I approached. "Find one you liked in there?" He thumbed at the back of the truck. "Not many left. This lady's ready to buy. You're about to lose your pup."

The woman shot a glance at me. "You wanted her?"

I bit my lip. "No, I'm really looking for a schnauzer. And this gentleman said he thought he'd be able to find one for me." I extended the piece of paper to him with a soft laugh. "I know this is unusual, but would you take my phone number? If you find what I'm looking for, would you let me know?" I sighed. "Remember, not a puppy. The more I think of my granny's dog, Gert, the more I love schnauzers." I scratched the ears of the poodle, dirt inching under my fingernails. "This one looks so sweet." I smiled and leaned in and whispered to the woman, "I've heard you can bargain and get a better deal."

She held the pup out at arm's length and winked an assent in my direction. "I'll try that. Thanks." She plopped the dog back into the cage. "Let me think on this before I buy. You'll be here all day, right?"

The man nodded. "But let's talk." He folded the scrap of paper with my phone number and tucked it into a pocket. "I'll give you a call soon's I know something." He spun around to face his customer and haggle dog prices.

I strolled away, happy the pup would get a new home away from the fetid cage, stopped in my tracks, and turned. "Oh, what was your name, sir, so I'll know when you call?"

He scuffed his boot across the pavement. "Joe. Name's Joe. Like I said, I'll be in touch soon." He reached in the poodle's cage and caressed the pup, his wheedling tone working the lady. I watched as he whispered something. Her eyes widened, and she took the matted dog while her husband fished out his wallet.

I retraced my steps and found a frowning Franklin, two cups in his hands. "What, may I ask, were you doing?" He held out a lemonade.

"I tried to encourage that woman to buy the poodle. It needed a good home." I sipped from the icy drink. "And I suggested she bargain on the price."

"And that's all?" He raised his eyebrows.

I grabbed his elbow and swallowed. I didn't want to needlessly worry him. "Well, I did buy pickles before I—"

"Hey lady!"

I cringed and turned as I heard the man's voice split the air. "Yes, sir?"

He tapped the crinkled piece of paper. "Is this number a seven or a one?"

Franklin stiffened.

"It's a one." I smiled and began to walk.

A hand clamped on my elbow. "Belle, what did you do?" Franklin hissed through clenched teeth. "Did you give that guy your phone number?"

A feeble laugh escaped. "Yeah."

"Whatever for?" Franklin swung around and stopped in front of me. "We were here to get information. Why would you give him your phone number?"

"I asked him to call me about a schnauzer." The lemonade soothed my throat. "I want to recover Schotzie. Ginnie needs to get that dog back." My lips quivered. "I only wanted to help her." *And pay my taxes.*

"Belle, do you realize if the guy has your phone

number, he now knows where you live?"

I frowned. "I didn't give him my address, Franklin."

"Yes, you did. In our new world, the Internet can cross reference a phone number with an address." His breath whooshed out. "With Google Earth, he can look at your whole neighborhood and spot your house."

Sweat tingled across my upper lip. I swallowed, my throat dry again. "He can?" I croaked.

"Yes, he can." Franklin stomped toward the truck, jelly jar tucked under one arm. "You're getting in over your head now." Grumbling to himself, people gave him wide berth. He shot a look at me. "And it's my fault."

"No, it isn't." I trailed after him. "I get into trouble on my own quite easily."

Franklin jerked the truck door open and helped me in. "Yeah, well tell that to Seth if anything happens." He puffed around to the other side and climbed in. "He'll blame me for bringing you out here." He slammed the door hard, making the truck rock.

"Then maybe it should be our little secret."

He glared in my direction and started the truck. Gravel spun under the tires as we exited the parking lot.

14

On the return trip, we made small talk, but once we were in my driveway, Franklin was quick to leave. He'd been irritated the whole drive home, reiterating my need for extra precautions now that the unsavory man had my phone number. I appreciated his concern yet grew tired of the scolding. I felt badly that I'd worried him, but what was done was done. I didn't know if I'd tell anyone about my encounter. Truth be told, I was a bit embarrassed at my stupidity. I should've known better.

My mind kept flitting to my deception over the next few days. Had I overstepped my boundaries? I'd probably never hear from that wonderful man again. That thought weighed me down.

In late afternoon, I drove out to the highway and cut over to a seldom-used dirt road winding through my property. Daddy and my brothers used to hunt nearby, in the section my uncle owned. My mom called it the back forty. Many a venison steak on our table came from these woods.

Leaning against the hood of the Jeep, I scanned the grassy pasture. Pampered Pooch was located nearer the highway. I could hear barks of dogs playing in daycare and smiled; then my heart jigged in my throat. My nose burned. I couldn't, I wouldn't lose this property. Too many happy memories had sprung from this soil.

I kicked a rut on the ground. I squatted and rubbed

the dirt-encrusted edges and spun to look at my tires. *Like I could track something? Get real, Belle.*

Still, the thief had to have a way of escape. Maybe they'd used this road instead of driving to the front of the kennel. And no way could Ginnie have spotted them.

I took a few steps toward the dog yard then kicked at the high-grown grass running down the center of the dirt road. Any vehicle coming through here would've left a trail of trampled grass. This hadn't been a recent escape route.

Disheartened, I returned to the Jeep. I sat in the front seat but didn't start the motor. I leaned against the headrest and ticked off ideas.

Mel. Angry at Ginnie and possibly Violet. Needed money. Good motives.

Darren. Messed up. Needed money for drugs. Motives there, too.

Jared. Angry teen. Period. Young enough to clamber over a windowsill and slip away during a dog show.

What else am I missing? Something was right before my eyes. . . .

Turning the Jeep around, I peered at Pampered Pooch in my rearview mirror. "Which one of you guys busted Schotzie out of that window?"

Work kept me quite busy the next week. With spring in the air, many clients added extra duties to my day. Even Donetta's list had grown. I didn't mind, as extra time meant extra cash, but my body felt the wear and tear. Before I left her house, Donetta asked if I could fit in "one more teensy little favor." I gritted and waited.

"My neighbor is in a panic." She sighed and fanned her face, perfume wafting through the air and nearly choking me. "Is there any possible way you could work for her? Family's coming and all. It would mean so much." Donetta's insincere smile gave me goose bumps. Still, I could always use the money. Especially now.

I flipped through my calendar and realized I could shift my day around, so I agreed and trekked next door. Donetta's neighbor, Carla Greene, gushed with thanks. "My in-laws are flying in from Michigan. This will be their first look at our new home, and I want them to be impressed." She shoved papers from the kitchen table. "Donetta raves about you and your work. Said you were the finest, most trustworthy maid she'd ever had."

I gritted. Donetta's maid. *Thank You, Lord, for another lesson in humility.*

"My son, Gabriel, will be home after school in just a little bit. His father picks him up. You may leave then. Garret will have a check for you." She dashed about the kitchen in circles. "I had a grocery list. Do you see it? Yellow paper."

I retrieved a yellow Post-it note from the floor. "This?"

"Oh, thanks. You're already saving my bacon." She squeezed my arm. "Thank you so much, Bella, for your help." She flew out the back door.

"Belle," I spoke to empty space. "My name is Belle."

I surveyed the cluttered kitchen. Not much was

dirty, but stacks and stacks of catalogs and papers were strewn about. No problem—I'd deal with it last. I found the cleaning supplies—nonorganic; Donetta would be upset—and headed up the winding staircase, toes in plush pile again. Same gold fixtures shone in the bathrooms and the same marble floors. Despite their owners' desires to be "all that," Lakeside homes seemed to be fancy cookie-cutter ones.

After a few hours, I heard a door slam and a scramble of someone coming upstairs. I stuck my head out of the upstairs TV room to see a gangly teenager.

"Hi, I'm Miss Belle."

"Oh, you're the new maid." He brushed past me to the computer. "Mom called my cell and told me you'd be here."

So much for manners. I unplugged the vacuum and glanced at the tracks Gabriel had just made. "You need to check the bottom of your shoes, please. You just tracked in mud."

He rolled one foot over. "Oh, man. It's poop."

I wrinkled my nose. "Then you need to get a paper towel and clean it up." I turned to exit.

"Wait. That's your job; not mine." He kicked a shoe in my direction.

"I don't think so." I shoved the shoe back with one foot. "I will vacuum this area again, but I will not clean your shoes."

He stood up and stomped his other shoe on the rug, a fine mess growing worse. "Well I'm not cleaning it up."

We were at a standoff. If this sniveling young pup

thought I was his *maid*, who would do his bidding much as a prince required, then he needed a reality check.

"You know, Gabriel, I am glad to help your mom get ready for your grandparents' visit, but I am not in the mood for your rudeness." I leaned against the doorjamb. "I could tell your folks about a couple of magazines under your bed."

His eyes grew huge. "You wouldn't."

I remained in place, arms crossed, lips in a thin line.

Within a minute, the young prince grabbed his shoes and marched toward the bathroom muttering. I was sure he wasn't using praise words.

"Gabe?" A man's voice filtered up the stairs.

I leaned over the banister. "He's in the bathroom."

"Hello, you must be Belle. My wife called me raving about your help." A dark-haired man peeked up at me. "I can't tell you how grateful I am." He sighed. "This unexpected visit of my mom and dad has thrown my wife into a tizzy." Rubbing his head, he said, "And it's so unnecessary. My parents aren't the least bit impressed," he swung his hands in a circle, "with all of this."

I walked downstairs. "I'm sure your wife just wants everything to be comfortable for them." *So the boy gets his rude gene from Mom.* "I'm going to finish up the kitchen now but wondered about some of these papers. Do you have a specific spot for them?"

Garret laughed. "If you could organize Garnet Jewel's paperwork, you'd be nominated for helper of the year."

"Garnet Jewel?"

"Our show terrier." He chuckled again. "Or my wife and son's show terrier. I just finance their shenanigans." He trailed after me into the kitchen and opened the refrigerator. "Want a soda?"

I nodded. "If you don't mind."

"Of course not."

We both popped a top, and I leaned against the counter, wondering how such a nice man ended up with a shrew and a brat.

The shrew entered a few moments later, crying hysterically. "Garret, come here." She wheeled about and fell into his arms. "Oh, Garret, what am I going to do?"

I watched the display of emotions run across the husband's face, panic winning.

"Honey, what's wrong?"

"Garnet's missing." She sobbed and threw a hand across her forehead, Miss Dramatic–style. "I picked her up from the groomer and left her in the car to pick up the cleaning." She wailed. "When I got back to the car, she was gone."

A tight white line formed around the man's mouth as he peered over his wife's shoulder. At the same moment, I heard a scream.

"You lost Garnet?" Gabriel wailed.

Visions of Linda Lester played through my head. I couldn't imagine dealing with the young prince and his hysteria.

"I'm sure she'll turn up. . . ," Garret began as his wife sank into a dining room chair.

"Mr. Green, may I speak with you a moment?"

I hated to be the bearer of bad news, but it seemed Kevin might need to come visit their house.

By the end of the day, weariness threaded its way through my bones. Seth called to chat. I filled him in on the latest missing dog, Garnet Jewel, and told him they'd called Kevin. He asked for their name and number so he could get a story started. "Think I'll come by for a visit this evening. You up for company?"

I eagerly took him up on his offer. Dish towel in hand, I swiped across the Formica and made a pitcher of tea. Seth arrived an hour later. I poured drinks, and we settled at the kitchen table for a visit. "How are things at the paper?"

He swallowed and dribbled some tea on his shirt. I handed him a napkin. "We've been really busy." Napkin in hand, he pointed at me. "Mom, another dognapping. Kevin said a poodle was stolen last week."

My hand trembled, and I set my tea down. "A poodle?"

"Uh-huh." He took another sip, and I waited. "A lady in Germantown. Kevin called me. Said she was really upset. Her son had just won championship points with the dog at the Memphis show."

Her son. An idea burned at the back of my brain. "How old was her son?"

"Teenager. I don't know. Why?"

I sipped and thought for a few moments then spurted out my idea. "I know this sounds weird, but do you know of the Internet site called MySpace?"

"Sure. It's an online meeting place." He pulled a bag of potato chips across the table and nibbled on one. "I've never used it, but I've heard about it."

"Well, I looked at it—"

"You were on MySpace?" He chuckled. "Whatever for?"

I cleared my throat. "Well if you'd let me finish."

"Sorry." He wiped his mouth and sat quietly.

"I visited the site after I saw some of my clients' kids online. And, Seth, every one of them has a MySpace account."

"Not unusual," he said. "I think a ton of teens do."

"True. But some of these teens had missing dogs, and those dogs were pictured on their Web pages." I watched his eyes as a flicker of interest grew.

"You think there's some connection between the Internet posts and the missing dogs?" He lifted his eyebrows.

"I think it's worth looking into."

"Let's go to your computer and check it out." He popped another chip in his mouth. "This is worth investigating."

We proceeded to the spare bedroom and turned on the computer. I dusted the monitor with a wadded up napkin as I waited for it to brighten. Seth hovered over my shoulder. "Do you know the name of the kid who lost the poodle?" I asked.

"Not right off hand, but it will be in my news story. We can pull it up."

I typed MySpace into the search engine and waited for the site to appear. When it did, I typed in Linda

Lester's name. I pointed at Schotzie when the picture came up.

"See? And the Clarence boys have their dogs on as well."

"Move a second, would you?" We exchanged places.

With a few clicks, Seth found his story about the missing animals online and scribbled the Germantown boy's name on an envelope. He flicked back to MySpace and entered the name. A connection flickered in front of us. Tod Ramsey and his poodle peered at us. I gasped. *I wonder if that's the dog at the flea market.* Leaning closer to the picture, I examined the dog carefully then straightened. No way to tell from the short time I'd seen the dog.

Seth read Tod's information and clicked a few connecting links. "I think Kevin needs to know about this." He swiveled in the seat. "Like you said, it could be a coincidence, but then again, who knows?"

"Honey, try Gabriel Green and his dog."

Seth entered the information, and there they were in color. The prince and his dog. I sighed. This was eerie. Seth pulled out his cell phone and walked toward the kitchen. I sat down at the computer and pictured a sad Gabriel Green looking for his terrier. My eyes welled with tears. He might be a brat, but he was still a child without a dog.

Seth left after his talk with an interested Kevin, who agreed to look at the computer site. I cleaned the kitchen and watered the outside plants. Restless, I called Ginnie. Charlie answered even though it was near ten o'clock.

"Hey, Miss Belle. Miss Ginnie's gone to a church meeting." His voice was muffled. "Hold on." I heard the slam of a door, and he came back on the line. "Sorry, I was putting up a dog. I can take a message and tell her you called."

"That'd be fine." My eyes widened. "Charlie, do you use the computer very much?"

"Yes, ma'am." He laughed. "I'm on it way too much according to my mom."

"When do you have time for the computer with your work schedule?"

"I don't work every night at the store." He blew out an aggravated huff. "I need to work more hours, but I don't get them. And since the hours I do work are weird, I don't sleep real good at night." He sighed. "That's when I get on the computer."

"Hmm, so I bet you use MySpace a lot."

Charlie snorted a laugh. "Definitely. I have a ton of friends on there," he said with pride.

"So I guess you can meet people from all over the place if you've got your own account." *People like dognappers.*

"Gee, I can't seem to get this rusty faucet open." Charlie grunted, and the thought crossed my mind that he was stalling for time. "Um, yeah, you link to other people and get to know all about them. But why are you so interested, Miss Belle? You looking to hook up with new friends?"

I didn't exactly know what he meant by hook up,

so I left his question unanswered. "I've got to get going, Charlie, but please tell—"

"Yeah, I'll leave Miss Ginnie a message that you called."

"Charlie, wait. One more thing."

I heard him breathe deeply. "Yes, ma'am?"

"Ginnie said you have a key to the kennel, correct?"

"I do."

"Where do you keep the key?"

Charlie paused. "On my key chain with all my other keys." His tone deepened. "Why?"

I peered into the distance, a tiny thought niggling. "I just wondered if anyone might've known you had a key to the kennel."

He sighed. "Guess so. I mean a lot of people know I work here." The faucet squeaked again. "I've gotta go, Miss Belle. I'll tell Miss Ginnie you called."

"Charlie?"

"Yes, ma'am?"

"Would anyone have access to your key chain?"

A long pause followed. "Well, my mom." He paused. "I don't know who else."

"When you're working at the supermarket, do you always have your keys on you?" I chewed on my thumbnail.

"Sometimes I leave them in my jacket pocket." He stopped. "But I never saw my key missing." Exasperated, he said, "Miss Belle, I've really gotta go."

"Thanks, Charlie." Placing the receiver in the charger, I headed to the computer again. In the

MySpace search box, I typed in Charlie's name. His site popped up, and I began to read more carefully. An entry called "My Typical Day" caught my eye. Charlie's embellished kennel job description would cause anyone to think he more than owned a key. And a key would be the ticket to Schotzie's freedom. I wondered what the sheriff's interrogation had ferreted out of the boy.

15

I tossed and turned Friday night, a gap-toothed dognapper racing through my dreams and Franklin nowhere in sight. I awoke with a heaviness in my chest as I remembered my deception. All morning I replayed our ride home and thought about Franklin's words. I'd essentially given the bad guy a map to me. A chill ran down my spine, and I plopped on the sofa.

Lord, You do protect the stupid, don't You? I feel awful about what I've done. Please forgive me. I glanced at the dead-bolted front door. It seemed secure. *And Lord? I pray for protection. Be my refuge.*

With that plea, I settled against the cushions and dug up my Agatha Christie book. My week had been full, and while I needed to clean my own house, it would have to wait. After my night, I needed rest more than a clean floor. The whir of the ceiling fan in the den drove me to a short nap after a few chapters. Yawning after forty-five minutes of slumber, I struggled to sit up. I couldn't remember when I'd felt so sluggish. And it was amazing the phone hadn't even rung. I rolled the kinks out of my neck, totally relaxed.

I heaved to my feet and headed into the kitchen trying to decide if I wanted to go for Chinese takeout or order a pizza. I ran my tongue across my lips. Lemon chicken or pepperoni? Dress and drive or delivery? Laziness prevailed. Which restaurant delivered? I pictured Theresa's garbage pile and saw the pizza name.

The phone directory under the cabinet even held a coupon. Victory was only a phone call away. Receiver in hand, I considered lemon chicken again.

The phone rang. Surprised, I tossed it onto the cabinet where it bounced to the floor. I grabbed it on the second ring.

"Hello, Belle?" Franklin spoke. "Did I call at a bad time?"

Giggling, I wiped my eyes. "No, not at all. I was about to make a call, and the phone rang. Made me jumpy."

"Oh, sorry. I'd never mean to scare you." He paused. "Well if you're busy—"

"No, Franklin, I'm not busy." I pulled a chair out from the table and sat, one knee propped up on the seat. I struggled to think of something to say. "What's going on in your life this Saturday?"

"Not much. I've kind of been lazy."

"Must be the weather. Me, too." I tugged my gown and slid it over one knee. I didn't dare tell him I was still in my night clothes at this time of day. My dream flickered through my head. "Franklin, I owe you an—"

"I know it's late notice," he interrupted, "but I have a hankering for some pizza, and I wondered. . ."

The giggle tirade began again. "I don't believe it."

"Don't you like pizza?"

I took a deep breath and filled him in on the events of the past fifteen minutes. I even went so far as to state I was still in my nightgown.

His deep rumbling laugh filled my ear. "Well, I'm

no better. So shall I pick up a pizza and bring it over, or do you want to go out to eat?"

I ran fingers through my hair and calculated the time it would take for him to order, pick up food, and drive to my place. I'd have time to be presentable. "Just come on over. I'll be here."

We decided to split a half pepperoni and half sausage large pizza, and he'd bring soda.

"Diet soda." I laughed. "Counteracts the calories."

"You've got it. See you shortly."

I hustled to my shower and washed my hair. Since Lorena's magic, my short style was quick to fix. I patted on foundation and eye makeup, squirted on some peach body splash, and then jerked hangers in my closet to find something besides jeans and a T-shirt to wear. My yellow summer dress and matching sandals made a cool comfortable outfit. Now if I could keep pizza sauce off the front of it. . . . I dug in my purse for some lipstick and spun in front of the mirror.

I stared at my reflection as a frown crossed my face. I needed to ask forgiveness for my deception. *Lord, give me the words.* I glanced at the clock on my bedside table and flew to the den.

I heard Franklin's truck rumble when I turned off the vacuum. I tossed the cord over the handle and shoved it into the extra bedroom. Fussing with my skirt, I met him as he rang the doorbell.

Pizza wafted in the door coupled with a sweet aftershave. I smiled. What a nice combination.

"Hey there." He lifted the box in the air. "Pizza guy."

I grinned. "Here, set the box on the stove, and I'll fix drinks."

Paper plates lay on the edge of the counter, so he served each of us slices of pizza. I nodded toward the den. "Let's eat in there."

"Or outside." He smiled. "It's a beautiful day I discovered, after I ventured outdoors."

"Then the front porch it is." I held the door open with my hip, and he went through.

He chose a rocker, and I placed our drinks on the small table in the middle. I sat and nibbled on a slice of sausage pizza. I dabbed my lips with a napkin and looked at him, willing the words to come. "Franklin, I need to apologize. My behavior at the flea market was wrong and I—"

One hand held up, he said, "Belle, all is forgiven. I was more scared for you than anything."

"I know." I sighed. "What I did was pretty stupid."

"I must admit, it was foolhardy." He sipped his drink and stared at me. "Just as long as you're safe. That's what's important." He raised an eyebrow. "That guy's not contacted you, has he?"

I shook my head.

"That's a relief." He set his glass down. "But keep on your toes. Be aware." He smiled. "And I'll keep praying."

I gazed at this kind, gentle man. "Thank you," I whispered.

"No problem." A short silence ensued. Then he pointed to his plate. "This pizza's really good."

"It is. One of Seth's favorites." I licked tomato sauce from my finger and glanced at my skirt. So far none had made it there.

Franklin chewed and rocked. "Nice kid. Bet he stays busy with all he has going on at the paper."

"Yes, he's a really nice kid."

"Doesn't he have a girlfriend?"

"No." Lauren's face flitted across my mind. "He dated a nice girl awhile back, but nothing came of it." I sighed. "She was such a sweetie, too."

"Guess you can't make choices for him now that he's grown." He chuckled. "Like my mom did for me."

"Really?"

"Oh, yeah. She had Kathleen handpicked, though I didn't know it for years. Kathleen's family and my mom's family went way back. Seems like we'd been destined for marriage before we were out of diapers."

"Do tell." I chewed thoughtfully. "Did it work out?"

"Yes. Well, yes and no." He sighed and bit off a dangling string of cheese. "Kathleen's job kept her busy. I was pretty absorbed in the farm. Never seemed like a good time to start a family." He wiped his mouth with a napkin. "We had good years, but we had some tough times in the beginning." He gazed into the distance. "I often wonder if we slid into marriage just because it was expected of us." He looked directly into my eyes. "Did you know Peter long?"

"Yes, we met in college." I took another bite.

"What about his family? Are they still in the area?"

I choked on pizza and began to cough. The patterns of this day were weird. I'd just thought about Phoebe, and now Franklin brought up the Blevins family? I held a napkin over my mouth, eyes closed.

"You okay?" Concern tinged his voice.

"Fine," I strangled out. I fanned the air in front of me and gave a watery smile. "A bite went down the wrong way." He handed me my glass, and I sipped. "Some of Peter's family lives in Trennan. His parents have moved. I don't have much contact with any of them. Seth sees them from time to time and on holidays." I hoped the subject was closed. That part of my life didn't conjure pleasant memories.

He nodded. "Holidays have been strange for me since my parents died." One foot pushed the rocker back and forth. "I have a couple of cousins I spend Christmas with now and then. But other than that, as an only child with no kids of my own, it could get pretty lonesome."

My face must've registered pity, because he leaned forward. "Oh no, don't feel sorry for me." His eyes lit up. "I spend Thanksgiving and any other holiday I'm alone working at the homeless shelter. It's such a blessing to give back. And when I see their plights, it surely does take the sting out of my life."

Lord, was Franklin created out of some special mold? Is he one of a kind? I've never met anyone like him in all my years.

"That's a pretty amazing attitude, Franklin."

He shrugged. "It's a God thing." He wiped his fingers and stood. "Want another slice? I do." He held the door waiting for my answer.

I shook my head. My clogged throat probably couldn't swallow.

Twilight settled in as we sat and talked. He told me Texas A&M stories and spilled some of their traditions.

I shared Seth stories and steered away from preacher wife ones.

The breeze filtered in sweet music from neighborhood kids squealing in their backyard. Peace filled me. The relaxing morning, a friendly dinner, the naturalness that came while being in Franklin's presence caused such contentment. I reveled in the moment.

Franklin said, "Guess I need to think about getting home."

I rocked.

"It's getting pretty late for a before-church night."

I rocked some more.

"What time does your church service begin?"

"I go to the nine o'clock service." I rocked.

He ran a hand across his chin. "Well, I can't join you in the morning because I have to meet with someone in my Sunday school class, but maybe another time?" He raised an eyebrow.

My heart started the flutter thing, and I rocked faster. "Sounds great."

He grinned, stood, and grabbed my hand. Pulling me to my feet, he squeezed my fingers. "Thanks for a great evening."

I leaned toward him, inhaling his cologne to make a memory. "You're very welcome. Glad to oblige."

He raised my hand and kissed my fingers then turned away. "I need to leave." His husky voice betrayed his emotions.

I licked my lips, missing the kiss I'd hoped was coming. "Good night."

He jogged to the truck and gave a wave before he

drove away. I watched until the taillights were pinpricks in the distance. He'd barely rounded the bend when a flashlight's beam stole across my front lawn. A light panned across me, and I shielded my face.

"Just making rounds, Belle, that's all."

"Thanks, Mel." I checked the dead bolt once I was indoors. Making rounds, or watching me?

16

Sunday afternoon my phone rang, awakening me from a deep sleep. After-church naps were the best.

Yawning, I answered, "Hello?"

A gruff voice said, "Is this the lady who wanted a schnauzer?"

Fear tickled my stomach, and my throat went dry. I clapped my hand to my forehead and sat up. "Yes, it is."

"They're hard to come by, searched high and low, but I got one for you. Want me to bring it to you so you can see it?"

Rubbing my cheek, I stammered, "Uh, no." My fuzzy brain scrambled. "I won't be home." *Great Belle. Tell him that so he can come rob you while you're gone.* "I'm going to the store in a little bit while my son works in the yard." *Just a little white lie.*

"What store? I can meet you there."

I put two fingers over my lips, then blurted, "The grocery in Trennan, on the square." I rolled my neck as tension settled in my shoulders. Franklin was right. I shouldn't have given the man my phone number. But in for a penny, in for a pound. And this dog might possibly be Schotzie.

"I'll be there in about thirty minutes and meet you outside." He hung up before I had time to reply.

"Oh, Lord, what have I done now?" I tugged at my shirttail and slid shoes on, heart pounding in my ears.

With shaky fingers, I ran a comb through my hair, staring at my pasty, white reflection. A sinking feeling hit my stomach, and I shot up one of my special frantic prayers. "I sure need protection, Lord." With a sigh, I headed for the back door.

As I grabbed my car keys and cell phone, I decided to call Seth. He'd be as angry with me as Franklin if he knew the full story, but I wanted someone to know where I'd gone. Punching in his phone number, I tried to think of what to tell him as I walked to the Jeep. Seth's voice mail picked up. Good. I would just leave a short message. "Honey, I am on my way to the grocery store in Trennan. On the square. I won't be gone long. I should be home in just a little bit. Please check in with me soon." Surely he'd be curious at the innocuous words, and he'd know where to locate me.

My anxiety about the meeting rose as I drove toward the town square. I chewed my thumbnail and fought butterflies in my stomach. I couldn't do this alone. I pulled to the curb and phoned Ginnie.

"I have a lead on a schnauzer. Maybe it's Schotzie."

"What? Where?" She gasped.

"Meet me at the square, and I'll explain. Hurry." I folded my phone and poked it in my purse. Drawing in a breath, I tried to steady my nerves. "Ginnie'll be there. Nothing's going to happen with two of us in a public place." I flung more prayers heavenward for protection.

At the intersection, I pulled to the curb and surveyed the store parking lot. Even on Sunday afternoon, a good number of cars filled the slots. Dennis, one of the bag boys, trundled in a row of shopping carts as several patrons loaded their purchases in their cars. The surrounding activity gave me a bit of confidence. Ginnie and I wouldn't be isolated. I glanced at the clock on the dashboard, my sweaty palms gripping the steering wheel. "Come on, Ginnie."

A familiar dented blue van crusted with mud passed me and swung into the parking lot. The beefy man sat in the passenger seat, a squirming dog in his lap. Joe had arrived. I watched as he circled the lot then stopped in an open area. Muddy tires. Maybe he had driven in the pasture.

My phone rang, and I jerked it from my purse. Ginnie's number showed on the display. "Where are you?"

"Did you find Schotzie?"

"Where are you? I need you here." Panic laced my words.

"I'm stuck. There's an overturned truck on the road." She sighed. "I hope I have enough gas to sit through—"

"You're not coming?" I squeaked, nausea creeping up my throat.

"Belle, I'm trying. Was that dog Schotzie?"

I looked at the van and kneaded my stomach. How long would he wait? My question didn't take long to answer. Joe began to creep forward out of the parking space.

"Look, Ginnie, I have an idea that the dog is in a guy's van here at the grocery store."

"How would you know?" she interrupted.

"I'll explain later." The van circled the lot again.

She let out an exasperated puff. "Well find him. See if it's Schotzie."

What had I gotten myself into? "Okay, I'm going to see what I can find out. Just get here as soon as possible." I placed the phone on the seat and noticed the van moving, this time closer toward the curb. I fought the urge to sink down behind the dash. I drew in a deep breath. "In for a penny. . ." Placing the car in gear, I pulled into a wide open space at the front of the parking lot close to the store.

When Joe parked I stepped out. He waved and walked in my direction.

"Hi, Joe." I gave a weak smile. "Nice to see you again. Thank you so much for meeting me here. And for going to all the trouble to locate a dog." I nervously prattled on. "This is such a pretty day, and to think I might be getting. . ."

His eyes darted to the van and back to me. "Found you a great dog. Like you want, a schnauzer. And they's hard to come by." He motioned at the other fellow with a jerk of his chin. "My partner didn't have time to give her a real good bath, so please excuse her mess. But she ain't a puppy." He wheezed. "Like you said, you wanted one house-trained. She's about a year old. I got her papers, and it tells her birthday." His gap-toothed grin gave me the willies. He flapped a sheet of paper in the breeze.

The passenger door opened, and a filthy animal shot out of the front seat, a rope tied around its neck. The end ripped out of the man's hand, and he bellowed at the dog. The pup headed straight to me. The schnauzer pawed my leg and whined. I knelt and scratched her neck. "Hey, puppy. How are you?" I whispered in her ear and held my right hand out palm down. "Setzen." The dog dropped into a sitting position. My pulse pounded in my temples. "Handschlag." She lifted her paw for a handshake. I gripped her dirty paw and wanted to cry.

"Whadda ya think, lady?" Joe sidled closer. "She's strong; that's for sure." He gave a wry chuckle and shot a disgusted look at the other man leaning against the van rubbing his blistered palm.

I swallowed, a knot in my throat choking off words. Schotzie continued to sit, paw extended. I slung one arm around the stinky neck and leaned back to keep from being licked. She trembled and whined insistently.

Joe picked up his spiel. "She's only five hundred dollars. Fair price for an animal like her." He flapped the sheet of paper again. "Papers and all." He snorted. "Tricks, too."

Heat flushed my face, and I clasped the dog to my chest, anger rising. Without thinking I blurted, "This isn't your dog." I jerked on the leather rope at her neck, a pigging string, and loosened it. The dog's head slipped free, and she scampered around my legs as I stood.

Joe stuck out a hand to catch empty space, then eyed his buddy and yelled, "Get that stupid dog."

Scooping up the rope, the man stumbled around, grabbing at thin air as the dog raced away in circles.

I whirled and faced Joe. "You're dealing in stolen dogs."

"Shut up, lady. You don't know what you're talking about." Veins bulged on his forehead as he lunged at the dog, his breath coming in short spurts. Schotzie dodged each man.

"Where did that dog come from?" The schnauzer headed to me, cowering behind my knees. I stood between the men and the dog. "I'm reporting this to the police."

The man started in my direction, and Schotzie bounded off. Joe's gap-toothed mouth curled in a grin, and he snorted. "You can't prove nothing, lady. This is my dog and my business."

"Want to bet?" I slid one arm around the dog's neck as she returned. I whirled toward the supermarket. "Security is right inside. Why don't we check?"

Joe's eyes widened as he looked at the plate glass window. A line of curious people watched. He waved at his partner. "Let's get outta here."

"But what about the dog?" The man grumbled.

"Forget it." Dashing away, Joe started the van's engine and glared at me as he waited on his partner. He shook a fist and shouted out of the window, "You shoulda kept your nose outta this lady." He stomped on the accelerator as his friend climbed in. I heard a third voice yell an expletive from inside the van.

"RD4150," I repeated over and over. Reaching in my pocket, I grabbed a crumpled receipt and pen to jot down the information. The grateful dog dove in across my body when I opened the car door, her stump of a tail wagging furiously. I slid in the driver's seat. "Schotzie?" A pink tongue bathed my face. "Stop it, stop it." I shoved her to one side and started the car. "Let's go see Ginnie and find out who you really are." My Jeep reeked of dirty dog.

Cell phone in hand, I called the sheriff's dispatcher and reported the van's license plate number then explained retrieving Schotzie as she twirled about in circles. "I believe the driver is dealing in stolen dogs." Schotzie jumped in the front seat of the Jeep and crossed back and forth, short barks expressing her delight. "Please contact Deputy Dawson. This is related to the break-in at the Pampered Pooch."

My next call was to Ginnie. "Turn around and meet me at the kennel." I didn't give her time to ask questions. I was too busy fending off a grateful dog while trying to drive.

Ginnie answered her front door with a screech when she saw the schnauzer. "Schotzie." She threw me a curious look and cradled the dog. "What happened?"

"She performed for me. I used the only German I've ever learned, and she performed on command." I followed them inside the kennel and walked straight to the kitchen counter to wash my hands. I wanted to scrub the doggie kisses from my cheeks but decided it could wait.

Ginnie sat on the floor with the stinky dog in her lap slathering kisses all over. "She looks terrible. She's lost some weight. But she's home!" She rolled her head backward to avoid the dog's mouth, giggling. "Oh, Schotzie-girl." Ginnie gasped and grabbed the dog's head to steady it. "When I talked to the vet about coming to speak, he said they kept records. Schotzie does have the microchip implanted." She filled a bowl with water and sat it on the floor. The trembling dog drank, splattering the tiles. "The vet will have a record of that." Her eyes gleamed with tears. "Oh, Belle. Where did you find her? I am so excited." She reached out to hug me. A sob caught in her throat. "Where was she?"

"In the supermarket parking lot."

She shot me a look. "You've got some explaining to do."

I sighed and sat at the dinette table. "Remember the flea market trip I made with Franklin?"

Ginnie nodded.

"I met this sleazy guy who had dogs—"

"A sleazy guy at a flea market?" Her eyes widened.

I gulped in a breath and blurted out the rest. "Ginnie, I told him I wanted a schnauzer, not a puppy, and gave him my phone number."

Ginnie shoved off from the floor. "Belle. Was that the guy you met in the parking lot? Are you crazy?" She raked her hair. "He might be the one who broke in here. He could've hurt you." She pointed at Schotzie. "For a dog?"

"A very special show dog," I whispered. I didn't add a word about property taxes.

She blinked back tears and paced around the room. "Did you at least report this incident?"

I nodded. No sooner had the words gotten out of her mouth than my cell phone rang. It was Seth. "Mom, what's up?"

Tears pooled in my eyes. My son would be frantic

if he knew what I'd done. I swallowed the catch in my throat and steadied my voice. "There's news on who broke into Pampered Pooch. I thought you'd want a lead on the story. Well, a possible story. Actually we're not sure this guy's the one, but it could be him. We'll have to find out more from Don, but we want to wait until we know for sure—"

He sighed. "Mom, are you okay? Have you been—"

I knew I was nervously rambling, so I swallowed the rest of my words. "Honey, I'm just fine. I'm with Ginnie right now, and we've located Schotzie." I gulped back tears. "Just wanted you to get the scoop after the sheriff does."

"Well, thanks, I guess." A beat of silence. "I'll contact Connors. Tell Ginnie I'll want to talk to her, too."

"Sounds great."

"Mom?"

"Yes, Seth?"

"I love you."

I sniffled and replied, "Love you, too, honey." I folded the cell phone shut, and tears cascaded down my face. Shivers ran through my body as the full realization swept over me. I'd been face-to-face with evil. And he still had my phone number.

After I calmed down, I described the afternoon's scenario to Ginnie. "That guy, Joe, and the one holding Schotzie—neither would've fit through the window." I walked down the hall to the storage room and peered up at the ledge. "They were both too fat." I ran my fingers along the windowsill above my head, black film coating them. "This has to be someone small enough to fit through that opening."

Ginnie leaned against the door frame, Schotzie propped against one leg. "They had to have help."

I bit my lip. I still hadn't mentioned my list of suspects to anyone. And I had no proof that any of them had committed a crime. "Did Sheriff Connors mention fingerprints on the gum or anywhere else?"

"Not to me." Ginnie scratched Schotzie's ears. "I want to call Violet Lester, but I'm going to wait until we have 100 percent identification." She flipped off the storage room light as I turned away from the window. "I know this is Schotzie, but still, the vet's office is closed on Sunday." Ginnie gnawed her lower lip. "But at eight in the morning, I'll be there with this pup. You can bank on it."

"I'll go with you," I said.

Ginnie lifted an eyebrow.

"Well, I want to know for sure if I found the right dog." As much trouble as I'd been through, at least I could see it through to the end.

"Okay, Belle. I'd appreciate the company." She looked at the dog, smiling. "I'm gonna give poopsie Schotzie a bathie wathie. She's all dirty. We don't want the doctor to see her that way, do we, honey?"

I grinned at my silly friend and prayed we truly held Schotzie. When Ginnie offered a cup of tea, I gladly accepted. My legs had suddenly become shaky again. The furious looks Joe had given me twisted a knot in my stomach. Maybe I had gotten in over my head now that I had stolen back the dog.

17

I arrived at Pampered Pooch by seven thirty the next morning. Ginnie had bathed the dog and covered her in fragrant flea powder. The pup lunged at me, her tongue looking for skin. I gently shoved her down, and Ginnie held her collar.

"Wherever she's been, she's been neglected." She ran her hand over the dog's haunches. "She must've been on the loose, because she's lost weight. It's a wonder she wasn't run over."

I kept quiet. Visions of the dog pens and filth filled my head.

She sighed. "Violet's going to be angry about the weight loss."

"Let's just pray Violet will rejoice because we do, indeed, have Schotzie."

"Too true." Ginnie slid her fingers from the leather collar and clipped on a leash. "It's not her regular collar—the rhinestone one is missing."

"I'm sure Schotzie will understand." I pulled open the front door and walked behind Ginnie and the dog. She slid the dog into a crate inside her car. The aroma of flea powder tickled my nose into a sneeze.

"You sure you want to ride with me?" Ginnie asked. "The smell might be a bit overpowering."

"Absolutely, I'm sure." I tugged a tissue from the center console and fastened my seat belt. "Let's get going. Curiosity is killing me." Not to mention the nagging worry.

The vet's car sat behind his clinic, so Ginnie pounded on the locked back door. Dr. Carlton opened it. "Mrs. Reynolds?"

Babbling, Ginnie pointed to the car and tried to explain what she needed. The doctor didn't seem to follow, so I walked over to clear up the conversation.

"We'd like to check to see if this is the schnauzer stolen from Ginnie's kennel. The dog belonged to Violet Lester. We understand the dog has a microchip."

"Of course. Bring the dog in before my first patient arrives." He held the door open and waited for us to retrieve Schotzie. A technician appeared in the hallway, and Dr. Carlton spoke to her briefly.

The dog was less than eager to see the vet and skittered toward the exit, her nails frantically trying to grip the tile. Ginnie teased her along to an examination room.

Once the shaky schnauzer was on the exam table, the vet probed and petted the dog until his assistant arrived with a file. He reached for a blue rectangular instrument about the size of a cell phone. The doctor held the wand and ran it over the dog's shoulders. "This is the proof we need."

I leaned in. "What are you doing?"

"Schotzie did indeed have a microchip implanted in her skin. I'm tracking it."

"Ouch."

"No, it doesn't hurt, and it saves a lot of hassle for the pet owner." He lifted loose skin between the dog's shoulders. "When Schotzie was brought in by Mrs. Lester, we slid a tiny transponder, about the size of a piece of rice, here. It has a permanent radio frequency that can be traced with this instrument." His eyebrows raised; the woman jotted down the number he called out and exited the room.

"She's gone to call the hotline."

Ginnie scratched the dog's ears. "What hotline?"

"The system I use is hooked up to a twenty-four-hour hotline. After a quick search of their database, they will identify the dog's number and match it to the owner." As we waited, he ran his hands over the dog's body. "I really believe you found the right dog." He smiled. "Mrs. Lester's brought Schotzie in numerous times."

I bit my grinning lip. As caught up in doggie world as Violet was, this dog probably saw a doctor as often as her children did.

The technician's tennis shoes squeaked into the room. "This is the dog you're looking for." She scratched Schotzie's neck. "The numbers on the chip match."

Ginnie started to cry. "Oh, thank you, Dr. Carlton." She pulled the dog's face near her own. The kissing began again.

I turned away and smiled at the assistant.

"How much do I owe you, Doctor?" Ginnie sniffled.

He laughed. "This one's on the house." He patted Schotzie's back. "Since you are going to have a teaching clinic at the kennel, we can use her as an example for responsible pet ownership." He turned to leave.

"Sounds wonderful." She continued to coo and pet the dog. "I'll call you with a date soon. And bring in a poster and some fliers. Thank you so much."

"I'd love to advertise." He nodded at both of us and left.

The technician lifted Schotzie down and gave her a treat. The dog skittered to the exit, tugging Ginnie along. I laughed and followed.

After loading the dog into the crate, Ginnie leaned against the car and sobbed into her hands. "Oh, Belle. Thank you so much. Thank You, Lord, for finding this dog." She took a deep breath and rummaged under her purse on the console for a tissue, then gazed at me. "Do you realize how relieved I am? I just knew Schotzie was dead in some research lab. And if word had gotten out, well, *when* word got out through Violet, Pampered Pooch's reputation would be down the drain." She wiped her nose and fingered under her eyes. "I must look like a raccoon."

We began to giggle. "Come on, Rocky Raccoon, I'll treat you to a donut on the way home."

"I have to call Violet," she said as she started the car.

"Uh-uh. Not until I've had a donut." I sighed and glanced at the dashboard clock. "I'm pretty sure Deputy Dawg is having his usual breakfast. We need to see him." It was time to talk to the law.

Ginnie and I wheeled into the Lester driveway after our donut break, the deputy following. Don said they'd not spotted the van after my call. I was disappointed and nervous. Joe in jail meant he'd not find me.

"I dread this." Ginnie looked at the front of the house.

I shook my head. "Uh-uh. You rejoice in this.

What was lost is now found." I grinned at the dog in the crate. "And they are going to be plenty happy. Brace yourself for hugs and kisses from Violet."

"Ew, no thank you," Ginnie laughed.

Schotzie sprang from the car and tugged Ginnie's arm. We trooped up the walkway onto the porch and rang the doorbell. Violet met us at the front door wearing a chenille bathrobe. When she saw Schotzie, she dropped to her knees and hugged the dog, tears welling in her eyes. Ginnie picked up, too. Dry-eyed, I felt out of place until Don sauntered up.

Violet batted her eyelashes and glared at Ginnie then swiveled to face Don. "She's in terrible shape," she sniffled. "It's about time you found her before she died." She stood up and took the leash. The dog pranced and jumped around her legs until they were tangled with the leash. I laughed, and Violet shot me a look.

"I'm grateful she's home." Ginnie nodded at me. "Actually, Belle found her." She wiped her eyes and placed her hand on the woman's arm. "Violet, I'm so very sorry this happened."

Violet jerked her arm away. "Me, too, Ginnie. At least it keeps me from having to deal with insurance papers. But you can be sure we'll take the dog with us next time we travel." Her mouth was set in a firm line. "Did you catch the thief?" She faced Don. "Where did you find her? At someone's house?"

I glanced at the deputy. "Miss Belle located the dog." Violet eyed me, and Don continued. "I'll explain, Mrs. Lester. May I come in? I have some questions for you, too."

"Well, we did offer a reward. . . ." She looked in my direction.

"Oh no." I held up a hand. "I don't want any reward. Why don't you help Ginnie with the clinic she's going to have at the kennel?"

Violet raised an eyebrow, and I nudged Ginnie.

"I'm having Dr. Carlton come speak one day soon. He's going to teach a clinic on being a responsible pet owner." She gave her sweetest smile. "As a matter of fact, he mentioned using Schotzie as an example of how well the microchip works."

A frown creased Violet's brow. "I don't know. . . ."

"The newspaper will surely cover the event." I nodded. "I'll have Seth come from Jackson. Think of the exposure for Schotzie and future pups."

A gleam flitted into her eyes. I'm sure it was made of dollar signs.

"I'll talk to Linda." She led the dog inside the house and motioned at Don to follow. "I think I need to care for Schotzie now."

"Yes, do that," Ginnie said. "Thanks again for being so understanding." The door shut, and we returned to the car.

"Belle, I'm so grateful." Tears welled in her eyes again.

I picked two donuts from the box on the floorboard. "Here's to returned dogs and lower insurance premiums."

Ginnie started the car, donut between her teeth, and we drove toward Pampered Pooch.

I called Theresa's house on the drive to let her know I'd be late to work and got the answering machine again. Determined to ferret out answers, I decided to circle by their house and see if I could see spotted dogs in the backyard.

No dogs were in the runs, but one of the boys was outside. John revved up their four-wheeler and headed out the gate and toward the ditch. A curtain blowing from the open patio door caught my eye. Jared leaned against the doorjamb watching his brother. Once John disappeared from sight, Jared turned in my direction. He jumped and slammed the door.

I picked up my cell and called the house. No one answered. Brat. I pulled my Jeep to the curb and trekked up the front walkway. He didn't answer my knock.

"Jared. I know you're in there." I rapped again. "I wanted to ask you about your dogs." Silence.

I huffed back to my car and sat there to see if he'd appear. After a few minutes, I decided I waited in vain. "But I know where you live, child. I'll be back."

I decided to call Seth before bedtime and 'fess up about the latest events. He could give Kevin the information from the license plate, and maybe it would lead to other dogs. Of course he'd have a conniption fit along the way.

18

Conniption fits over the telephone aren't nearly as bad as they are in person. Seth had fumed and fussed, coming short of calling his mother stupid. I'd apologized and promised my investigation was at an end. He had all of the information about the van, took my description of the men, and said he'd call Kevin.

"Mother, I promise you, we are not finished with this discussion."

I grimaced. His tone of voice mimicked one I'd used with him more times than I could count. I stopped short of relating my suspicions about Mel, Jared, and Darren. He'd rant more about Belle-the-investigator, and I wasn't sure I wanted to hear it.

I replaced the receiver in its cradle and leaned against the kitchen counter, eyeing the back door. That creep Joe had my phone number and could find my address, and now I'd antagonized him by snatching Schotzie. Would he come looking for me?

Goose bumps rippled down my arms. I reached for the doorknob and checked the dead bolt, then walked through the living room and did the same on the front door. The knob was locked; the dead bolt wasn't. I snapped it in place. For sure I'd have to be more vigilant, pay more attention.

"Being in for a penny sure has consequences," I muttered. But maybe I'd saved a few pennies in the long run.

That evening I cut up lettuce and tomato for a salad to counteract the donuts I'd eaten for breakfast. Surely the calories would balance out. I didn't even use dressing, just a hint of lemon. After peeking out the front window and seeing no Mel, I took my dinner on the porch and sat in the breeze while I ate. My first bite of the beautiful tomato was a letdown. I'd be so glad when the first round of fresh summer fruit and vegetables came in. Nothing reminded me more of summer and relaxation than a fresh tomato. Kind of like Pavlov's dogs.

A truck came into view. I chewed and watched as it approached my drive, curiosity slowly drowned out by a jolt of fear. When it rounded the small curve, I could tell it was Franklin. I patted my mouth with a napkin and set my salad on the small end table. My heart pitter-pattered in its regular rhythm. I glanced down at my raggedy jeans and T-shirt, wishing I'd changed after work. Too late now. I finger combed my hair.

He parked and mounted the porch steps. "Belle, good to see you."

I stood. "I'm glad to see you, too." I motioned to the chair. "Have a seat."

The rocker creaked as he sat. "Heard a little story today from Kevin." He frowned in my direction. "Just thought I'd pop in and check it out."

Heat crept up my cheeks. "Would you like some tea?"

"Not right now, thanks." He rocked back and forth, the creak comforting in the twilight. "Want to give me the real version of what went on?"

"Real version?" I sipped from my glass.

He smiled. "I'm learning there's a bit more to Belle Blevins than meets the eye." He stopped the chair. "Or should I say 'Investigator' Blevins?" He shook his head. "I cannot believe you met that man. Scared me to death when Kevin told me you'd snatched that dog back." He gazed at me, his voice easy but steel-edged. "What were you thinking? Remember our conversation about unsavory characters living in this county?"

I chafed under his stare and grew uncomfortable. Then aggravation crept in. Who was he to fuss at me? I'd had enough of that from my son.

"Whoa. Wait a minute, Franklin," I sputtered and straightened in my chair. "I admit that not all I did was smart, but I chose to give out my number in hopes of finding Schotzie. And that worked out just fine, thank you very much."

He ran a hand over his eyes. "Okay, I'll give you that. The dog is home safe and sound." He eyed me for a moment.

I leaned back in my chair. "I know, I know. I tend to get overinvolved. Don't think I haven't had this lecture from Seth." Rubbing condensation from the tea glass, I peeked up at him. "I'm sorry for being foolish. Guess I owe you that much."

His voice softened. "You know, I enjoyed our time together, and I was worried sick, afraid I'd gotten you into trouble the other day."

My edges softened. "I'm sorry I worried you, Franklin." I sat up straighter, trying to look the part of in-charge. "I'm a bit rash at times."

He chuckled. "From what I hear, that's an understatement."

"Now wait a minute." The ire rose again, and I sat my glass on the table. "I'll admit from time to time I get a bit curious and—"

Franklin reached out and took my hand. His warm calloused fingers closed around mine, warming me to my toes. "Belle, I'm just praising God you're safe. I'm glad your friend has her dog back, but I'm so grateful you're okay." He squeezed my fingers. "Let's just drop the fussing. Tell me what happened."

Fingers intertwined, I gave him the abbreviated version, watching my tennis shoes as I talked. "I was smart enough to meet them in a public place, and there was store security." I peeked up at him.

"I'll give you credit for that." His thumb rubbed a tiny circle on the back of my hand, making it hard for me to concentrate. "Never thought you were a dummy." His lips tilted up.

"But we still have no leads on who burglarized Pampered Pooch."

"We?" One eyebrow rose.

I held up a hand. "The sheriff." I could see there was no point in reciting my list of suspects and risk another conniption fit.

He glanced at my unfinished salad. "Guess I've interrupted your dinner."

I nodded, then flushed. "I could fix you a salad if you're hungry. Might even have some chicken to toss in."

"Not an imposition?"

"Not at all."

"Sounds delicious." He stood and tugged me to my feet, his fingers squeezing mine a moment before he let go. He tipped his head and tapped my nose. "Belle Blevins, do not ever scare me like this again." His voice dropped to a whisper. "You've gotten under my skin, lady." His eyes twinkled. "Let's make a salad."

Dazed, I followed him into the kitchen glad we weren't in conniption fit territory. I rather liked this new terrain.

He found the remaining salad in the refrigerator and filled a bowl. Pouring ranch dressing over the top, he licked his fingers and sealed the bottle. "Any tea left?" He filled a glass and nodded at the door. "Let's go outside, and you can finish dinner, too."

I grabbed a packet of crackers and trailed behind. We sat in our rockers and continued dinner in silence, the crickets' cry beginning in the twilight. Peace washed through me as the familiarity and ease of our visit continued.

When we finished our last bite, Franklin insisted on washing the dishes. Seeing those tanned hands plunged into soapy dishwater made me grin.

"What?"

I giggled. "I bet you aren't used to washing dishes in the sink instead of a dishwasher."

He flicked suds at me, and I jumped back. "Wrong. With just me and the dogs, I seldom use a dishwasher. And my sink sometimes collects dishes." He held up the bottle of soap. "I do use a brand that's a bit gentler on the hands." He squeezed the bottle, and tiny bubbles escaped, not unlike the bubbles about to burst within my heart.

Dishes dried and put away, we meandered into the den. He scanned the photos on my mantle and picked up one of my parents. "Tell me about your folks. Are they still alive?"

I shook my head. "We lost Daddy to a heart attack when Seth was a baby." I sighed. "My mom struggled with Alzheimer's, and she died last year."

"I'm sorry to hear that." He set the picture down.

"What about you?"

"My mom died a year ago. She lived in Nashville. She would've been ninety-four next February." He laughed. "She was a tough old bird. Lived on her own. Kept driving until she had an accident three years ago." He shook his head. "I had to lay down the law and take her car keys then."

"It's hard parenting your parent." I plopped on the sofa and pulled a pillow in my lap. He sat beside me. "Mother lived with me the last few years, and I had to lay down the law some, too." Memories tugged, and I smiled. "We had a few good arguments, I can tell you that."

Franklin looked at me. "Things haven't been easy on you, have they?"

I felt a tingle in the back of my throat, but I would not give way to tears. His sympathetic glance pricked the dam, and one slid down my cheek. "No," I choked out. "Things haven't always been easy." I fingered the pillow's edges and glanced at the front door.

"Is the dead bolt locked?"

I felt heat rising in my cheeks. "Yes, I checked it earlier." He raised an eyebrow. "And the windows," I added.

He sighed and tilted his head toward the ceiling. "Please keep my favorite girl safe, Lord. Despite her, keep her safe."

I tipped my head back and said, "Despite me?"

He tapped my nose again. "Yes, despite you, Miss Investigator."

Franklin left a little before nine, pleading a long workday. I walked him to the truck, where he grabbed my hand. "I've sure enjoyed this evening."

"Hmm, me too," I murmured.

"Want to repeat the process?" He grinned.

I squeezed his fingers. "On one condition."

Franklin held me at arm's length. "Condition? What condition?"

"No more scolding." I smiled. "I have Seth to fuss at me."

He chuckled. "It's hard to keep from fussing over one you care about." He climbed into the truck. "But I'll try to accept the conditions."

I waved and stayed in the driveway until the taillights were pinpricks in the distance.

Floating back to the house, I locked up then leaned against the kitchen door. I smiled at the dish-washing liquid bottle. I needed to find out what brand he preferred.

I pulled on a nightgown, dried my hair, and then slid into bed, the covers up to my chin. I snuggled against my pillow. "Lord, I never thought I'd feel this way again," I whispered to the darkness. "I thank You for keeping me safe, and I thank You for a wonderful new friend." I paused, eyes closed, chewing my lower lip. "And who in the world climbed in the window of the Pampered Pooch?"

I'd just about hit dreamland when my phone rang. "Miss Belle?" A tremulous voice said.

"Who is this?" I hit the switch on my bedside lamp; the digital clock read twelve thirty.

"Jared. Jared Clarence," he whispered.

The comforter slid from my shoulders as I sat up. "Son, what's wrong?"

"I need to talk to you but not over the phone." He paused and lowered his voice. I cupped my hand against the receiver to hear. "I can't talk now. Can you come back by my house tomorrow afternoon?"

I agreed, and he hung up. Was I about to receive a confession?

19

As soon as I finished at Hannah's, I would swing by and find Jared. He'd not be home from school yet anyway. I parked my car in front of the Johnson home because Darren's car was still in the driveway. I sent up a plea for direction and stepped to the back door.

A rushed Hannah answered my knock. "I'm running late as usual," she huffed. "Darren is gone, so you can lock up when it's time to leave." She grabbed her purse and jerked her chin toward the table. "I left your check."

"I saw Darren's car out front." I twisted my purse strap around one finger.

She nodded. "He's out with friends but said he'd be gone all day. I forgot to tell him you were coming."

A flicker of relief ran through me. I wouldn't have to deal with the creepy kid.

Hannah paused, doorknob in her hand. "Thanks for the prayers, Belle. He's been a lot nicer to live with lately. We had a long talk about the baggie, and it was empty. He swore he's not into drugs." She smiled. "I appreciate your concerns."

A slice of guilt shot through me. *Judging again, Belle.* "I'm glad to hear it. I'll keep on praying."

She waved as she slipped out the door.

"Thank You, Lord. I'm glad she's seeing evidence of prayer." I began to hum as I walked toward the master bedroom. "Holy Spirit, draw this family close to You."

I changed the linens on Hannah's bed and tossed them into the hall. I'd carry the dirty clothes to her washer in the garage before I left. Tugging the vacuum across the old carpet, I began to recite the suspect list with each swath. Mel, angry. Jared, sneaky but ready to admit his wrongdoing? Darren, improved? Charlie, available. Hmm, a new thought.

My concentration wavered, and I switched to prayers then dusted furniture. *Sure wish we could clean our sin life away as easily as furniture polish gets rid of dust.* With one finger, I wrote Franklin's name inside a heart across the coffee table then swiped it clean. A grin tugged my lips. I hadn't done that since high school. I whistled and hummed my way around the room.

I scoured the bathrooms and headed toward Darren's room. Towels and T-shirts littered the floor, but I made short order of those, adding them to the pile in the hallway. I laughed at the screen saver when it danced across the monitor. It was a picture of Darren and his mother on a Christmas morning. *How sweet. Maybe he's a nice kid after all.* The guilt niggling died down.

Inside, I beamed. Surely my prayers had helped. I tapped the computer mouse, but only the desktop icons appeared. I chewed my lower lip, toying with the idea of checking his MySpace account, but decided to leave it alone. With a contented sigh, I continued to clean his room, praying over each surface.

The pile of dirty clothes in the hall had grown, so

I used a towel to collect as much as I could carry. With one hand, I opened the kitchen door into the garage and tossed out the bundle. I returned for the last few sheets.

I stepped into the dim garage to slide the pile in front of the washing machine. The only light came from the three windows across the top of the garage door. Dropping my last load, I bumped against the dryer.

A leather jacket slid from the top. I grabbed one sleeve with my hip before it hit the ground and pulled it in front of me. *Mighty hot for a leather jacket this time of year.* I fingered the collar and read the label. *Whoa. This is expensive.* I held it up for closer inspection. I glanced around the garage and saw a stack of boxes.

"Oh, Darren's stuff from school." I folded the jacket over my arm and looked for a hanger to hang it on the rod above the dryer. Something dangled from the pocket and slapped against the dryer. I slid my hand down to catch whatever it was and gasped. A pigging string.

I flung the coat on the dryer, string in hand. The unmistakable small, soft rope with the waxy texture formed a loop through a steel eye. On the end of the rope was a piece of rawhide that kept the rope from fraying. I fingered the string. Small gray hairs peeked from the fibers. Hair that looked remarkably like dog hair. Like Schotzie's.

I shivered. My mind raced. Darren's drug use had to be fueled with money, and the grocery store didn't pay that much. Had he gotten involved. . . ?

The rumble of the garage door opener overhead

made me jump. I grasped the string to my chest and swirled to go inside. My foot tangled in a sheet, and I tumbled to the laundry pile. I struggled to free myself before anyone entered the garage.

Too late. I looked at two pairs of legs standing next to me. I recognized Darren's tennis shoes, but the other boots weren't familiar.

"Miss Belle. You okay?" Darren reached down to help me up. I flailed and tried to stuff the string under my shirt, but the rawhide hook caught on a shirt button. It jerked free.

Boot-feet leaned down and picked it up, and the stench of tobacco hit. When I rose, I stood face-to-face with Joe. Panic riddled me. My heartbeat's tempo raced, and I stuttered, "Hello, guys."

Darren unwound the sheet from my left leg. Joe's jaw clenched, his mouth a grim line. He leveled a glare at me then turned to Darren, holding the string in his face.

"Look what your cleaning lady has found."

A flush ran up Darren's cheeks. "I thought I lost that." He reached for the pigging string, and Joe jerked his hand back.

"Idiot. She knows what it is." He leveled his gaze at me again. "Don'cha, lady?"

My voice quivered, "I've seen some like it. When I was younger, I went to a lot of rodeos. My brothers used to. . ."

The look in his eyes shut me up. Shrill barks sounded from outside. I could see the front grille of Joe's filthy van behind Darren's car. Another shudder ran down my spine. They had more dogs.

"Belle cleans our house, Joe. She's no trouble." Darren touched his shoulder. "Let's get outta here."

"We ain't going nowhere without her." Joe thumbed at me. "She knows too much."

Darren blanched. "Miss Belle? What does she know?"

Joe leaned into Darren's face. "She knows plenty, stupid." He shook the string in my face. "You saw this Sunday. You called me a thief on the same day, remember?" He cut a look at Darren. "This was the lady I took the dog to on Sunday."

Wide-eyed, Darren started to move his mouth, but nothing came out. He stared at me then finally blurted, "But we can't take her."

I faced the boy, willing him to be right.

"Want to bet?" Joe snarled.

Suddenly my body was engulfed in a blue sheet. I batted at the fabric as it settled about my body, but Joe had a grip around my waist.

"Open the van door," he said.

Darren protested again as Joe dragged me out of the garage. I dug my shoes against the concrete, but one hard jerk from my captor freed them. I kicked Joe's shin. He grunted and gripped me tighter. His tobacco odor filtered through the fabric. "Lady, don't make me hurt you." I kicked again and fought to rip the sheet away, twisting my shoulders and jerking my head. Joe's knees met mine, and I buckled. He half carried, half dragged me another few feet.

His voice came in short spurts. "Help me out here,

Darren," he gasped for air, "or you'll regret it."

Darren lifted my shoulders. Joe's hands slid down my legs, and I felt the pigging string slip over one ankle. I jerked and kicked, but Joe must've had plenty of practice. Soon I was bound. Still I flailed my elbows, slipping from Darren's grip. I screamed at contact with the pavement.

A hand connected with my cheek. The sting made me bite my lip, and I tasted blood. "Shut up!" I smelled Joe's stinky breath through the cloth as he knelt in front of me. "We're taking you out of here," he said through gritted teeth, "so cooperate, or you'll be sorry."

Tears coursed down my cheeks. I leaned against the sheet and wiped my face. "I won't go with you." *Yeah, like you have a choice, hog-tied and wrapped in a sheet.* A flare of anger burst through my chest, and I screamed, "You are a thief and a kidnapper. You won't get away with. . ." My world went black.

Pain radiated through my scalp, down my neck and shoulders, and into my back as the van bounced down a highway. I licked my busted lip. The bleeding had stopped. Sweat stung my eyes. Tires hummed against the pavement. Tied around the waist, hands at my sides, and my feet bound, I slithered to one hip. I wished Hannah's sheets weren't so dark. My feet bumped something, and a dog barked. I scooted and touched the edge of a cage with my fingers then felt another.

The van swerved. I heard gravel crunch, and my

head slammed the floor as we flew over the next rut. We'd hit a country road. I rolled to my back, the better to take the brunt of the rough ride.

Tears slid down my temples. I wanted to blow my nose. I wanted to sit up. I wanted to see. I wanted. . . *Jesus, help me. I'm so scared. Jesus, help me.* I created a tune in my mind and sang the words over and over. Calm washed through me, and the tears stopped. I rolled back to my side and nuzzled the sheet, drying my face. A puppy whined.

"Shh, baby. We'll be okay," I whispered. "Jesus will watch over us." Confidence flickered through me.

The van jolted to a halt. I heard Darren and Joe in the front seat.

Darren whined, "Joe, she ain't going to be a problem."

"Look, kid, this is my operation, and we'll do things my way." He spit out the words. "So you'd better get used to the idea."

Darren tried again, and I rooted for him to win.

"You want your money?" Joe snarled.

Silence filled the van, and I knew I'd lost. Drug money willed out.

The front doors clicked open and slammed. I heard the side door slide open. We must have reached our destination. Had I reached my end?

20

Darren pulled me to a sitting position and slid the string from my feet. He whispered, "I'm sorry, Miss Belle. I never meant for this to happen." He loosened the tie from my waist and pulled the sheet off my head. I sucked in fresh air and looked the boy in the eyes as I ran my hands up and down my arms.

"Darren," I hissed, "you need to get out of this operation now before anyone gets hurt." I wanted to scream "before I get hurt," but one look at the frightened kid's face frozen in shock made me realize his vulnerability. "This guy's dealing in bad stuff." Tears welled in my eyes, and I brushed them away.

Darren nodded and helped me stand. "I know." He shot a look over his shoulder. "I'll get you out of here. I promise."

I stood beside the van on shaky legs, eyes blinking to adjust to the light, Darren's grasp on my elbow oddly comforting. We had parked before an old kudzu-covered farmhouse on a gravel driveway. Weeds covered the area except where tires had cut a recent path. A wreck of a barn sat behind the house, weathered boards pulling away from the sides. I spotted an old rusted tractor under a layer of weeds and green. Stagnant rainwater sat in a muddy hole near the porch. No one had worked this place in many a year. Swiveling my gaze, I tried to figure out our location. A crick stabbed my neck.

A dog barked. Inside the van were four stacked cages each holding a beautiful, cowering dog.

"More assets for Joe?" I cocked an eyebrow. Darren flushed. "This is wrong, son." I tugged on his sleeve and spoke through clenched teeth. "You have to call for help."

Joe swung around the front of the van folding a cell phone. "Why did you let her loose?" He thundered at Darren. "She didn't need to see anything."

I glared at him. "Like I recognize where we are." I waved one hand. "This could be Timbuktu for all I know."

"Shut up, lady. You got a big mouth." His hand lifted, and I flinched.

"Wait, Joe." Darren jumped between us. "She's right. She doesn't know where we are. Let's just leave her here. Nobody's been in this direction for ages, 'cept us. And we're almost through at this place."

Joe ran his hand over his chin and peered at the boy. "Maybe you're right. She gets hurt in an abandoned house, ain't our fault." He sighed. "Got to move her car though." He ground his boot into the gravel and let out a string of curse words. "Never planned on this." He glared at me again. "Stupid lady. Why you gotta be so all-fired nosey?" He spat and walked to the house.

At the moment, I wondered the same thing.

Soon the rumble of a generator filled the air.

Darren squeezed my elbow. "I'll play him along, Miss Belle. I'll find help for you." He tugged me toward the house. "I am not a killer."

Tears blurred my vision, and I batted my eyelashes.

"Thanks, Darren." I swallowed a lump in my throat, my heart's rat-a-tat almost drowning out words. "I've been praying for you."

The boy dropped my arm and stopped short. "Praying for me?"

"Yes. And for your mom." I gave a watery smile. "I know things haven't been easy for either of you." Tears stung the back of my nose, and a few leaked down my cheeks. "But this isn't the way you want to spend your life. We only get one time around, son, and the choices we make affect others, too. Be smart, Darren." I gulped and whispered. "Don't do anything stupid."

He nodded, and we continued to the house. My hips hurt from the rough ride, and I gingerly took the three steps up the porch. The front door stood open. Through a ragged screen door, I saw a table with a computer and two lawn chairs in the empty living room. Joe stepped outside and held the door open. "Home, sweet home, Miss Belle. Don't even need you to clean up."

I shuffled inside. A screen saver danced across the laptop's monitor: Pampered Pooch's advertisement. They had Ginnie's computer. I gasped.

Joe's tobacco-stained chin lifted, "Yeah, we needed better equipment." He sneered, and his laugh sent chills rippling down my back. "Take our guest to the basement." He clapped a set of handcuffs into Darren's hand. "Use these."

Darren and I walked to the kitchen. I stumbled over peeling linoleum and peered at the rust in the sink. Definitely no one had been here for a long time.

At the basement door, I hesitated. "I can't go down there," I whispered, my fist clenched against my stomach.

Joe saw me stop and charged into the kitchen. "Yeah, lady, you can." He reached over Darren's shoulder and shoved. I toppled to the third step. "It's going to be nice and quiet. Just you and the spiders." His cruel laugh tied a knot in my stomach, stirring up the queasiness. My legs quivered as I tried to stand.

Darren scrambled to the bottom. "I'll leave the light on, Miss Belle." His voice soothed me as he pulled the string on the lone bulb.

I descended nine more steps to the filthy floor on shivering legs, my arms tucked around me. Shelves surrounded the basement, a few jars sitting here and there. Dirt encased most of the one window on the back wall. Spiderwebs hung from rafters and beams. The swinging light cast shadows in the corners, and I didn't want to know what lurked there.

Panic roiled in my chest, and my breath came in gasps. Sweat beaded on my upper lip and trickled down my back.

I threw a pleading look at Darren. "Don't leave me here." A sob tore from my throat.

"I have to for a while, Miss Belle." He motioned to a furnace. A steel girder held it in place. "Sit down here. You can lean against this."

I shook my head. "I can't."

"Miss Belle," Darren whispered, "it's either me hooking you up or. . ." He jerked his head upward. "And he'll be a lot rougher, believe me."

I cocked my head and heard someone enter the front door. Could help have arrived already? No, Joe was talking to the other person. Probably the hulk that had been with him in the van.

Nausea won over, and I darted to the corner. The breakfast I had earlier splattered over the floor. I cried, deep exhausting sobs ripping through my body.

"What's going on down there?" Joe shouted.

"She's sick." Darren pulled my arm and whispered, "Sit down before he comes."

I pulled my T-shirt up and wiped my face then dropped to the floor grasping the boy's blue jean leg. "Darren, you have to get me out of here." I battled a scream.

"I will." He squatted and clapped the handcuff on one of my wrists and attached it to the girder. He squeezed my fingers and straightened.

"Thank you, son," I sniffled.

He patted my arm. "When Joe gets ready to leave, I'll figure out a way to stay here and cut you loose."

A shuffle at the head of the stairs caught our attention, and Darren paled.

"Well, that would be stupid, Darren."

Panic constricted my chest. Charlie Baker glared at us.

"Charlie?" I squeaked. He'd made it on my suspect list just in time.

He sneered at me. "Yeah, Miss Belle. Charlie." He blew a pink bubble and let it burst, the pop punctuating the stillness. "Charlie the pooper-scooper. Charlie the put-it-on-the-shelf boy. Charlie the wash-your-own-clothes son." He gave a nasty laugh. "It's

Charlie the money-making man now." He nodded at Darren. "Those furnace pipes make great speakers. Get up here, stupid. We've got some talking to do." He wheeled and left my sight.

Trembling, Darren shot me a frightened look and climbed the stairs. The door closed. I heard the front door slam, then silence.

The smells from the shut up basement were overwhelming. I burrowed my nose against my knees and tried to pray. Tears soaked my jeans. I was so scared, I couldn't form coherent thoughts.

Jesus, Jesus. The word resonated through my heart.

───

Time passed, and I dozed, exhausted from the adrenaline rush. I opened my eyes, grateful the lightbulb still flickered. I tugged at my restraints but nothing moved. I jerked violently and bruised my wrist.

Running my free hand over my grit-covered face, I leaned against the girder. Who would find my car? Who knew my schedule? Hannah knew I'd been there. Maybe she'd see my purse. I frowned. If Joe remembered my car, he'd get my purse out of the house, too. I peered at empty dog cages piled under the stairs. Evidently he'd made a living out of stealing and covering his tracks.

A veil of despair billowed over me, and tears threatened. My head pounded, a migraine-nail stabbing my left eye. I shifted positions and drew my knees close to my chest to rest my head. Crying, I gasped, "Oh,

Jesus. I'm in a real pickle." Despite myself, I chuckled. *A pickle in a basement.* A sob caught in my throat. "What in the world do I do now? What will they do to me?"

I pressed the heel of my hand against my eye, willing the throbbing pain to lessen. Focusing on the bottom step, I began deep breathing Lamaze style. Those childbirth classes many years ago still had benefits. I massaged my neck and tried to relax lest nausea overtake me again. Time dragged. I dozed.

When I awoke, my feet were asleep. Rubbing them helped some, but I needed to change positions. I knelt. Stinging needles pricked my arches. I swiveled around and sat, tapping my toes. The stinging sensation began to disappear. I stretched my legs and bent at the knees. Any exercise would help restore the circulation. I floundered around, twisting and turning as best I could.

I tapped my feet, this time pointing my toes and making circles. I set up a cadence. The rhythm began to calm me, and I hummed. Soon a song broke forth. "Standing on the promises of God my Savior. . ." My voice rose in pitch. I could never carry a tune in a bucket as my dad said, but the spiders didn't seem to care.

The words of the hymn caught at my heart. Had I been standing on the promises or growling at them? My anger at God had intensified once Peter drove away. I spent a good deal of energy floundering through scriptures to find my new direction. But had I forgiven Peter? Really forgiven him? Did I still harbor anger and bitterness in that junk drawer? I gnawed my chapped lip. I'd recently told Franklin my bitterness was resolved.

"Lord," I spoke into the dank room, "help me in my unforgiveness. I'm weak and You are strong. Your Word says You will never leave me or forsake me." I reeled off another promise. "You will provide for my every need. And I need to get out of here." My voice dropped to a whisper. "If there's any area, Lord, where I need to forgive, please point it out."

Phoebe's face whirled in front of me. Blond and blue-eyed like her older brother, she had adored him. And had been so unkind when Peter left me. I wrinkled my brow. Could it be she'd been so embarrassed by her perfect brother's behavior that she'd lashed out at me? In turn, after his death, I hadn't been the best ex-sister-in-law, either. I did call and visit his parents, but it was on Seth's behalf, not to assuage their grief. My head pounded, an aura flickering about my eye.

The grocery store flashed through my mind. Phoebe and I had approached each other in the produce aisle. I saw her first and wheeled my basket in the opposite direction, but she caught my attention.

"You still working in the cleaning business?"

I'd detected a note of disdain. "Yes, it's going fine, thank you."

Her lips pressed into a thin line. "My mother-in-law might have need of your services. She's not doing so well."

"I'm so sorry to hear that." I fished in my purse for a card. "Here's my number. Call me, and I'll check my schedule." I walked away.

And that wasn't very long ago.

Guilt washed over me. "Oh, Lord. Help me to forgive Peter's family, especially Phoebe. Cleanse my heart, Father. Make me like new. Give me the chance to tell Phoebe I love her and to help her mother-in-law." I lowered my head to my knees and prayed like never before. Tears stained my already stained jeans.

In a while, I lifted my head and relished the cleansing I felt. No matter what happened, my relationship with God had grown. I continued to sing praises. Hymn after hymn poured out of me until I was hoarse. I longed for a drink of water.

My knees ached. I evaluated the angle of the girder and handcuffs then stood. Bent at the waist, I shuffled and squatted a few times. *Keep the circulation going, old girl.*

The lightbulb flickered. Another knot of panic tightened as I watched it dim and then brighten. "Oh Lord, please keep the light on." No spiders had skittered over me, but I didn't want to sit in the dark. No sense giving them a chance to weave me in a web.

I stomped my feet and sat Indian style. "Okay. Now what do I do?" Talking aloud seemed strangely calming. "Okay, let's see, can I still recite the names of the state capitals?" I tried a few but gave up after five. "Scriptures, then. That should help." I recited the Twenty-third Psalm and Psalm 100. "Thank you, Mrs. Bass, for teaching me to memorize those in Sunday school." I squinted, trying to remember another. "Proverbs. 'Trust in the Lord with all thine heart.' Boy, is that ever a timely one." I kept up my monologue.

"Well, you have no other audience, so just blurt it out." I paused. "I really like Franklin. He's a fine man, and he was so right about me getting into trouble." I grinned. "I hope I get to kiss him." I rubbed my nose on my knee. "Keep going, girl. Blurt it out, Belle. You always keep things bottled up. Just blurt it out." I gave a sour laugh. "Yeah, right. You never keep your mouth shut; that's why you're in this predicament. Seth, you are right, too, I'm a trouble magnet." I snorted. Laughter bubbled up, and I gave way to a fit of near hysteria. Again, tears threatened, so I sang.

The room dimmed as twilight fell and light from the window paled. I trembled. Night in a Tennessee basement. I shuffled around and jerked on the girder. It didn't budge. I was so thirsty my tongue stuck to the roof of my mouth. My lower back throbbed. I really needed a bathroom.

I tried to find a comfortable position. No telling how long I'd have to sit. No telling how long until I lost consciousness. No telling how long. . .until I died.

I leaned back and closed my eyes, picturing Seth. My handsome boy. Peter and I had been married two years before the Lord gave us Seth. The day he was born, I had whacked Peter's back and hollered, "Call the doctor; I'm in labor." He groaned and rolled over in bed. We'd been to the hospital with false labor two days before. This time I knew the difference but had to convince my husband. A knee in his back did the trick.

Peter drove like a madman, running three stoplights. Where were policemen when you needed them? We slid into the emergency room parking lot like a runner hitting home plate. Peter didn't wait for anyone. He jerked a wheelchair from the lobby and raced to the car. A startled nurse met us at the ER doors then grinned. "Ready for this baby, Belle?" I groaned, clutching my bulging belly and looked at my beautiful neighbor, Judy, sure she was an angel.

Labor only took seven hours, and I was wheeled into the delivery room. I'd tried to be the brave pioneer mom and dispense with medicine, but after a few hours of searing contractions and deep breathing, I hollered for drugs. In those days, we hadn't had the luxury of birthing while someone else told you a contraction was on the way. Uh-uh. You felt every one of those puppies. Crests of pain, then exhaustion as you waited for the next wave. No, Demerol was my friend after a while.

Seth Peter Blevins entered the world howling, a head of downy brown hair and scrunched up navy blue eyes. His father's chest puffed out so much I thought he'd explode. He held our son in one arm, a hand trailing down Seth's cheek, touching his fingers and toes.

"He's perfect, honey. God's given us perfection in a blue blanket." Peter's tears rolled past his beaming smile.

Tears flowed again as I thought of that precious moment. Peter had been so in tune with us. A real family unit. Unshakable, I thought. Where. . . I caught myself. I wasn't going down that rabbit trail ever again. If I got out of here—no, *when* I got out of here—my relationship with Peter and the worries I carried about what I'd done wrong would be buried forever.

I bit my lip. Did Seth know I was missing? Was he looking? Probably not. We didn't talk daily, and he had no reason to know I wasn't at home. The despair veil floated across my eyes, and I shook it off with a song. "Bless the Lord, O my soul, and all that is within me. . . ."

I was not giving up. Not yet.

A shout rang out, "Miss Belle?"

21

D arren?" I shot to my feet, wincing at the needles pricking my sleeping toes. "Where are you?" Hope flared.

"I'm upstairs," he groaned. "Cuffed to the drain-pipe in the kitchen."

"Oh, honey. Are you okay?"

He puffed a short laugh followed by another groan. "As okay as I can be with my skull split open."

I slid to the floor and faced the furnace. Our conversation floated through the connecting pipes. "What happened, Darren? I thought you left."

"No, Charlie used me to help unload the dogs and go get your car. Then he conked me on the head and dragged me in here." He sighed.

I must've really slept deeply for a while. I never heard them.

Darren said, "Don't know where he got another set of handcuffs." I heard the clink of the cuffs against the pipe. "And there isn't any give in this pipe." Frustration bit at his words. "I can't get loose."

I chewed on my lower lip. "Can you saw back and forth? It might cut the PVC."

"Nope. It's old metal pipe. Won't work." The cuffs clanked again. "See, won't loosen." He paused. "But you know what?"

"What?"

"I did get a call through to my mom's cell."

My eyes blurred with tears. "Oh, Darren. She's coming?"

A heavy sigh and a sob brought me up short. "No. I got her voice mail, and all I said was 'Help.' I punched in 911, too, but then Charlie was coming, and I hung up."

"Where's the phone now?" My insides pleaded for the right answer.

"I don't know. In my jacket somewhere. . ." His boots scraped the floor; then discouragement filled his words. "Not in here. Under the porch."

Hope plummeted. I bit back words of anger and disappointment. No good in those now.

"I'm sorry, Miss Belle." Darren sniffled then cried in earnest. "I'm so, so sorry."

I closed my eyes. *A little late for that, son.* "I know you are, Darren." My soothing mom tone came natural. "Calm down." Here's the preacher's wife's encouraging words. "It's going to be okay. We'll get through this."

"How can we?" His sobs carried through the pipes. "I've messed up so much. How can it be okay? My mom's gonna be worried sick. Again. I keep worrying her over and over." He hiccupped. "I'm just no good. I should've run away like I planned."

Shifting positions, I gathered thoughts to quell this fever of despair. "Darren, you are wrong. You are good. God sees you as good."

"Ha, yeah right. Like God sees me at all."

"He does see you, Darren. In the Bible, it tells us He sees us before we're ever born. While you were still in your mom's tummy, God saw you."

"What are you talking about?" he asked, confusion filling his tone.

Lord, give me words to speak to this child. Calm my fears, and keep us in the palm of Your hand.

I drew my knees up and took a deep breath. "Darren, God created you, and He even knew we'd be together on this very day in this old house." I nodded, my heartbeat slowing, ministering to myself. "This is no surprise to God."

The floor squeaked as Darren shuffled about. "I don't understand."

"I know." I smiled. "So let me explain."

He strangled out a laugh. "Not like I've got something else to do."

I cleared my dry throat. "Then since we've got all this time, let's make good use of it." I gripped my temples and squeezed to ease the headache's tension then started. "We all do things we shouldn't do, and the Bible calls that sin. When we want to be a part of God's family, we have to get rid of the sin."

"Ha, can't do that."

"No, *you* can't. Not on your own." I sighed. "Just listen."

"Okay, I'll listen."

"God knew we wouldn't be able to keep from messing up, so He sent his Son Jesus to pay the price of our sin."

He shot out a laugh. "Even mine? Stealing dogs? Smoking dope? No, that can't be right. You don't do anything that bad."

I snorted a laugh. "In the Bible, there's a story of a man named David. God called David a man after His own heart. Well David slept with a married woman," I paused for effect, "and killed her husband."

"And God still liked him?" Darren's question squeaked.

"Incredible, huh? It's called grace, Darren."

Darren moaned. "I've heard about that. My granny used to say she wanted me in heaven with her." He let out a huff. "My granny used to sing songs to me at night." He sniffled. "I really miss her."

"Darren," I said, "you can see your granny again in heaven. All you have to do is ask Jesus into your heart." I waited for his response. *Lord, You brought us here for such a time as this.*

Scraping sounds signaled Darren's moves. "I'm on my knees, Miss Belle."

I grinned. "Why?"

"My granny always prayed beside me, and I had to be on my knees."

I leaned my head against the post and closed my eyes. He'd had a praying granny. *Thank You, Lord, for those who keep on praying for us.* "Then let's pray."

He parroted the prayer I said; then he laughed. "What else do I do?"

Tears rained down my face. "Normally, you'd hug me, but that's a little hard to do in this position, isn't it?"

He bit out a sob. "Yes, ma'am. But I'm not as scared." He shuffled around. "Miss Belle?"

"Yes, Darren?"

"My granny used to sing to me. I dreamed awhile ago I heard her singing again. Could you sing some Jesus songs for me?"

I thought of the cross-faced man who'd glared from

the computer screen, the air of disgust surrounding Darren. And I listened to the gentle words of a sweet new baby Christian asking for music. He'd heard my joyful noise as he lay unconscious above me, of that I was sure.

"Yes, Darren, I'll sing some songs for you." I started with "Jesus Loves Me."

———

Darren shared bits of his life after our song session. "I just got greedy. And stoned." He groaned. "When I moved into the dorm, I was on my own. So cool. Mom had smothered me growing up. I know she didn't mean to—don't get me wrong. But man, I got so tired of her questions and being all over me after my dad left." He quieted. "Then at college, marijuana flowed. My roommate shared some with me. My first taste of the wild life." He paused. "Man, you could score weed anywhere, and I did. I think I stayed high for like a month."

"Is that what got you kicked out of school?"

"Oh yeah." Bitterness tinged his voice. "I got busted. Stupid, stupid me. I got busted. Weed practically grew on campus, and they caught me? Talk about a setup."

"What do you mean?"

"Steve, my roommate, was a jock. He registered late and didn't make it into the jock dorm, and he wanted a friend of his to room with him. Well, campus said they wouldn't make changes. So I think he made the change for them." He laughed. "Guess who his roomie is today?"

"His friend?"

"You got it. Ain't fair, is it?" He moaned. "I never had the cash for the amount of dope found in my backpack. He had to have stashed it."

"I'm sorry. . . ." I caught myself. "I'm sorry you got framed, not that you got caught."

"Yeah, I know."

"How'd you get in the dognapping business?"

I heard the exasperated huff of air. "Charlie. When I started at Greeley's, he buddied up to me. I asked him about scoring some dope, and he turned me on to his dealer."

"Charlie?" I squeaked. "Charlie has a dealer? Does he use dope?" I visualized the clothes washing scenario. Maybe his mom wasn't allergic to dog hair but had a sensitive nose for marijuana.

"Yeah, Charlie, and yes, he smokes. They upped the price, and I needed more money. So Charlie offered to pay me for dogs."

"How does this operation work?" I scratched my nose and pulled up my legs Indian style. "Did you help find dogs?"

"I'd been on a Web site called MySpace at college a lot."

I chuckled. "Believe it or not, I'm familiar with MySpace."

"Wow, Miss Belle. I'm surprised you know about it."

Another kid thinks I'm older than dirt. Gee, thanks.

He cleared his throat. "You meet tons of people online. One day I looked at a site that belonged to a neighbor kid. John Clarence."

"I work at their house. You saw the dalmatians on John's site?"

"Yeah, I did."

"Was Jared Clarence involved in all of this?" I remembered the late night phone call.

"Charlie tried to involve him. Took him to a dog show 'cuz he knew a lot of people there. But he was too scared to be of any use to Charlie."

Maybe the trip to Memphis had been his downfall. Good for Jared.

"Back to MySpace. You collected friends on your page?"

He snickered. "You have been online."

"Imagine that."

A beat of silence, then he continued. "That's when I got the idea about the dogs. I knew a lot of other rich kids around Trennan and Jackson and found the information about the mutts on their sites." An expletive flew out. "Kids that rich should be smarter."

I frowned at the language. "Guess so. But let me just tell you, they aren't all that rich. And none of them deserved to have their pets stolen." I pictured Charlie in the kennel kitchen as Don questioned him. He'd looked so innocent. "How long has Charlie been doing this?"

"For over a year. He and Joe went to Virginia to a dog show before I met him. He told me about it. They even broke into some trailers and stole stuff. He said those rich people would never notice it gone; they all had insurance." He groaned. "And I took the bait. I set up about five dogs in the last few weeks."

"Sure did hurt some hearts." I thought of Susanne and her missing Yorkie. Joe and Charlie had probably been in Memphis. "The Clarence boys were quite upset over their dalmatians." Hope rose. "Do you know where the dogs are? Did they go to fighters or research labs?"

"No. The ones I took Joe were sold. He said he'd get more money because I chose good dogs." He snorted. "Least I was good at something."

I ignored his remark. "Did you know about the schnauzer Joe tried to sell me?"

He barked a laugh. "Well, I didn't know it was you at the time, but yeah, I knew about the schnauzer. That was one of the first deals I was in on."

My forehead wrinkled. "How did you get Schotzie out? Didn't all the dogs go nuts?"

"Charlie fed 'em all treats. So while they munched, we made tracks with the dog."

"Who climbed in the window?"

"The window?"

"The window in the storage room had been. . . Charlie," I whispered.

Darren coughed. "Yes, Charlie made it look like a break-in. Even the gum. He said he used gloves so no fingerprints would show up." He snorted. "Like he was some crime expert."

"We returned Schotzie to Linda Lester. She's the owner." I sighed.

"Yeah, I was in the back of the van when Joe peeled out of the parking lot the day you got the dog. Almost knocked me out."

I remembered the sounds of a third person in the van. Gnawing my lower lip, I wondered. Maybe Kevin could track down the pets. At least they hadn't gone to slaughter. I scooted to another position, my feet tingling.

"Miss Belle, I hate the dark."

I swung my gaze to the dirt-encrusted window. "Is there not a light up there?"

"No." The little boy voice returned.

I licked my lips and glanced at the lone bulb spilling weak light. "Darren, can you reach the basement door? You turned the light on in here."

The scrabbling and scraping that followed made me wonder what contortions the boy tried. I watched as the doorknob twisted a tiny bit. Then suddenly the door flung open.

"I did it." His exhilarated squeal made me laugh.

"You did. Do you have some light?"

"I do." He gasped. "Almost broke my wrist, but it isn't so dark up here now. Thanks, Miss Belle. Good idea."

"Hey, Darren, let's practice thanking God." Silence met my statement. "Darren?"

"I've got light, but I'm not out of here yet."

"True. But we're to be thankful in all things." I closed my eyes. I needed to remember that truth, too. The words of the doxology flowed off-key from my parched lips. "Praise God from whom all blessings flow." My throat clogged.

I was tired, sore, and scared. Bolstering Darren had held my faith steady, but exhaustion threatened to pull me under its waves. "Darren? Are Charlie and Joe coming back with more dogs?" A shudder tickled my spine.

"No," Darren said with finality.

My eyes widened and my stomach clenched. "They're not?"

"No." His boots scraped the floor. "Charlie told me on the way here they'd dump you and find another place to use."

I gasped. No telling how long it would be before anyone would step foot into this farmhouse. From the bouncy ride, I knew we'd covered a good bit of territory outside of the city limits. I fought rising panic.

God, I told Darren You knew where we are. Help me. Give me strength and faith.

"Well, son," I said, "guess we'd better start praying for rescue."

"I'm pretty tired, Miss Belle." He sniffled. "I'm sorry."

"I know, Darren. Just rest, and I'll pray."

I closed my eyes and talked to the Father. Sleepiness washed over me, and I shifted positions to rest my head on my knees. A smile played on my lips. If this were to be my last day, I'd know the boy in the kitchen would meet me in heaven some day.

Seth's face loomed. I lifted my head, and tears coursed down my cheeks. I wanted to see my son. Proud as I was of Darren, I wanted to live and see my son. Would I? Or would the green icing kudzu cover our coffin in layers?

22

A sunbeam tapped my eyelids open, and I squinted at the window. The lightbulb glimmered. *If I ever get out of here, I want to know what long-lasting brand it is.*

I couldn't believe night had ended. It had lingered forever. Hope rose then plummeted. So what if it were day outside. That didn't bring help any closer.

I slid my feet under me and stood. Everything ached. Anger burned through my hungry stomach, and I jerked the handcuffs against the pipe.

"Miss Belle?"

"Sorry, Darren. I didn't mean to wake you," I croaked, then shuffled my feet in a wake-up dance. "I am just tired of sitting. Did you get some sleep?"

I heard a yawn. "Yes, ma'am. I did." The floor creaked, and he stomped his feet. "I'm tired of sitting, too. And I'm so thirsty." He coughed. "I pulled on this pipe till I cut my wrist. But ain't no give to it, and no water in it either."

Self-pity welled up alongside my anger. "Well, if you'd chosen a better place to handcuff me, maybe I could've gotten loose."

My words hung in the air.

He moaned, "Guess I didn't think. I'm sorry. Again."

I crossed my legs and plopped down, my anger deflating. "I'm sorry, too, Darren. You didn't know." Forehead in my hand, I felt the tears burn my nose. "Let's pray, okay?"

"Yeah, I'd like that."

I led us in a prayer and tried my best to be upbeat. But fear gripped my heart and ripped at my faith. *Promises. I have to grab hold of promises.*

"Darren," I struggled to inject some enthusiasm into my voice, "did you know scripture says God is faithful to all His promises?"

"Really? So what did He promise for this situation?"

I caught the cynical undertone. "He promised He'd never leave us. So He's here right now." I gulped. "No matter what, He's here right now." Tears tickled my cheeks and dripped from my chin. "No matter what, Darren. Remember that." I choked back sobs.

The sun's angle told me time passed, though it seemed a crawl. I licked my lips and dreamed of water. I thought of the ice cold bottle Franklin had pressed into my hands at the dog show.

His hands. Beautiful long fingers, perfectly manicured. How could he work in dirt and keep his hands so nice? I looked at my weathered, dishwater-wrinkled hands. I'd have to learn his secrets.

I hitched a breath. If I ever saw him. . .

Stop it, Belle. God is faithful. Don't give up yet.

I hummed a praise song. Praise kept the devil away, my mama always said. So I'd go to my grave praising.

A door slammed, and I shot straight up. They were back. Charlie and Joe had come back. Bile rose in my throat, and I trembled. Footsteps echoed above me. *Well, Lord, it's show time. Show us what to do.* I bit my lip and waited. Would they deal with Darren first, then me?

"Mom?" Darren's croak sounded out.

"Darren!" Hannah screeched. "What's happened?"

Hannah? How in the world. . . ? "Hannah. It's Belle. Down here. Help," I squawked through tears.

Hannah's feet beat a rhythm down the steps. "Oh, my word. Belle. What's going on?" She stooped beside me and rubbed my chafed wrist. "How do I get you loose?"

"How did you find us?" I sobbed, falling against her chest.

"Darren's cell phone." She glanced at the stairs. "He's handcuffed, too. How do I get you loose?"

"Call the sheriff." I shuffled to my feet. "Call the sheriff and ask for Don. Tell him to call Seth." I rubbed my hand across my face.

She gripped my elbow and nodded. "Don already knows. He and the sheriff are on their way." She looked at the stairs. "I'll be right back."

"I'll be here." I gave her a wry grin. Dropping to the floor, I wept and praised a faithful God.

———

Deputy Dawg was a sight for sore eyes. He and Sheriff Connors thundered down the steps, ordering Hannah outside. Another deputy wielded wire cutters and freed my wrist. I drooped against Don's waiting arms.

"Hang on, Belle." He hugged me to his broad belly and helped me upstairs. His donut-stained shirt never smelled so good.

Seth and Kevin stood outside near the sheriff's car. Three other patrol cars lined the driveway, lights flaring in all directions. A string of yellow tape was pulled across the doorway, and I ducked under it, racing to my son's arms.

"Mom." Seth's voice wavered, and I sobbed against his shoulder.

"Miss Belle." Darren headed in our direction with a tearstained face. "Miss Belle, I'm so sorry."

I held out a hand, and he grasped it. I whispered, "It's okay, brother." I squeezed his fingers. "You're my brother in Christ now, remember?"

He gave me a watery grin and nodded. "I can't believe you're forgiving me so fast."

"You're forgiven, Darren. And not just by me." I kissed his grimy forehead and slid my arm around Seth's waist. "Now I need to know how in the world Hannah found us."

Kevin smiled. "Darren used his cell phone to call his mom." Kevin cut a glance toward Hannah and raised an eyebrow. "When he stayed out all night against the house rules. . ."

Hannah clutched Darren around the waist. "Sheriff Connors discovered he'd also called 911, although he hung up before it was answered."

Darren nodded. "I tossed it under the porch before Charlie saw it."

"The sheriff had arranged with his mom earlier to set up this sting." Kevin placed one hand on Hannah's shoulder. "She knew he'd been sneaking out and assumed it was to purchase drugs."

A flush crept across Darren's face, and Hannah looked stricken. "I only wanted to protect you, son." She squeezed him.

"So when he hadn't appeared on time again," Kevin continued, "she told Connors. He arranged a GPS trace, and your location was recorded."

Hannah gripped her son's arm. "I was so afraid you'd gone back to smoking dope, and I wanted to catch you before it was too late."

Darren grinned. "For once I'm glad for that over-protecting mom."

We all laughed as Hannah hugged Darren.

Kevin continued, "The dispatcher gave Hannah the location, and she beat them here. She wasn't supposed to be here." He frowned at her. "It's a good thing the patrol car was following close behind. What if you'd found trouble?"

A flash of uncertainty crossed her face; then she faced Kevin like a mama bear. "I came after my son. Any mother would've done the same." She interlaced her fingers with Darren's.

Kevin clamped his mouth closed but not for long. "I was sure surprised when Don called me." His brooding eyes aimed in my direction. "He found the only relative I have who sniffs out trouble like a bloodhound."

I rubbed my aching arms. "So the minor detail of a cell phone rescued us?"

"Yep, Belle, guess you could say so."

Daddy, you were right. It's the details that trip 'em up.

Leaning against Seth, I said, "Take me home. I think I need a bath." Wordlessly, Seth hugged me.

A deputy stepped forward. "The sheriff said he would talk with you later, Mrs. Blevins, for your statement." He turned to Darren. "Son, you're under arrest."

Hannah gasped, and Darren looked me in the eye. "It's okay, Mom. I'm ready to face the truth." He reached out his arms to the deputy.

The kind man shook his head. "I think you've had enough handcuffs for a while. Just climb in the back of the squad car. Your mom can meet us at the station."

As they walked away, I whispered, "Thank You, Lord."

Kevin crossed his arms. "Aunt Belle, you've wiped out another legion of guardian angels, I do believe."

Seth pressed his lips against my hair. "Come on, Mom. Let's get you home."

"Better words were never spoken." I slid into Seth's car and sighed. *Lord, God, there is no end to my gratitude.*

23

After a long shower, some painkillers, and plenty to drink, I let Seth wrap my strained and bruised wrist in an Ace bandage. He pointed me toward my bedroom, where I slept most of the day, awakening to see him pace back and forth in front of my door. "Shh, go back to sleep, Mom." He motioned with one hand. "You need your rest. I told Don we'd talk to him tomorrow." He stepped to the bed and tugged the covers over my shoulder. "I'm watching over you, young lady, so rest."

I snuggled deeper into the comforter and drifted away, not even a Franklin dream filtering through the exhaustion, aches, and pain.

By 5:30 I awoke starving. The aroma of spaghetti wafted through the air. I smiled. Seth had made his only dish just for me. I slipped on my robe and padded into the kitchen, running my fingers through my squeaky clean hair. Ah, clean, a wonderful feeling. No spiderwebs left.

"Hey, you feeling better?" He reached out and hugged me closely. I held on. Never had his embrace dissolved my insides so. I shivered and felt a sob creep up my throat. My legs quivered. "Shh, Mom, it's okay." He leaned his chin on the top of my head. "It's all over. You're home safe and sound."

"I know." I sniffled and reached for the dish towel on his shoulder. "I'm still amazed at that thought." I cupped

Seth's face in my hand. "Oh, honey, I thought I might not see you again." The torrent of tears began, and my child held me as I cried. Spent, I sagged against him.

"I've been praising God all afternoon, Mom." His eyes sparkled with unshed tears as he tapped my chin with one finger. "I'm blessed to have Arabelle Blevins as my mom; but boy, you can scare me." He shook his head and hugged me. Then he gulped before he spoke. "I do have some news. The sheriff caught the bad guys."

I leaned back to peer into his eyes. "He caught Joe and Charlie?"

"Yep." Seth led me to the kitchen table. "With Darren's guidance and the license number of the van, they were able to track them down." He poured me a glass of tea and slid a plate of spaghetti across the table. "You could use something to eat, I bet."

I toyed with a noodle. "So explain the scenario." I slurped spaghetti, though my stomach rolled and rumbled.

"After he got to the station, Darren confessed his part in the whole dognapping operation." Seth sat down, his plate full. "He also gave a partial description of another house they'd used to stash dogs." He chomped on a bit of garlic bread, and I waited. "They weren't very smart. Franklin had told Kevin about the flea market expedition," he said, "which we can discuss later." Seth's frown censured me, and he took a sip of tea. "Kevin relayed that information to Deputy Don. Working with Connors and a map, Darren retraced some of the moves they'd made." He settled back in the chair. "Shortly after you and I got home, Don and two other deputies followed the circuitous route and busted them in Joe's own backyard." He shook his head. "They were ignorant enough to head back to their own lair."

"What about the dogs?" I croaked, my throat still stinging.

Seth smiled. "There were two caged dalmatians for sure. And it seems the Newfoundland had been sold locally. I'm not sure what others they recovered."

Tears welled in my eyes. "I pray they got them all. I was so afraid that scum Joe was into dog fighting. He seemed the type."

"He was. Animal control captured several pit bulls he'd been training." Seth propped his elbows on the table.

"I still can't believe Charlie was involved." I sighed. "Ginnie will be sick when she finds out."

"She already knows."

I drew in a sharp breath. "What about Darren? Will he have to go to jail?"

Seth shook his head. "I don't know all of it, but the sheriff said there would probably be some kind of plea bargain for his testimony." He took my hand. "Darren told Don about his newfound Christianity due to one captured woman." He squeezed my fingers. "Preaching to the handcuffed—does this mean a prison ministry in the making?"

"No, not yet." I smiled. "How did Ginnie find out?"

"I called her." Seth pointed to my plate. "Eat some dinner, Mom. You have guests coming over in a bit."

I slid spaghetti in circles and took a few tentative bites. After a sip of cold tea, everything tasted better. I ate enough to keep from hurting Seth's feelings then returned to my bedroom and pulled on a loose-fitting sundress. Nothing to touch the bruised and battered areas of my body, please. I retrieved aspirin from the bathroom cabinet and popped two in my mouth. Thankfully, a migraine had passed me by.

Seth hollered, and I walked to the living room, where Ginnie yelped and grabbed me around the waist.

"Oh my word, Belle. You almost died." Tears and mascara dotted my clean sundress. "Are you okay?"

"I'm fine, Ginnie. Really, I am." I sank to the couch. "It was a frightening experience, but the Lord brought me through."

She sat beside me, one hand holding mine. "This whole charade began because of me." She sniffled. "If anything had. . ."

I patted her hand. "But it didn't, Ginnie. God protected us." I smiled. "I bet I used up a whole legion of guardian angels these last few hours." I tipped a look in my son's direction. "At least that's what the police told me."

She and Seth both laughed. My laughter surfaced, but it didn't touch my heart. If they only knew the fear I'd been through. I shuddered as the dank-smelling basement flickered through my mind. Despite hot water and soap, the smell lodged in my memory.

Ginnie talked to Seth about the return of the dogs and Violet's apology. She mentioned the upcoming vet clinic she would host at the Pampered Pooch. Seth suggested ideas for an article. I had a hard time concentrating on their words, and it must have shown.

"I'm tiring you out." Seth wandered into the kitchen to avoid possible torrential tears, and Ginnie reached for her purse. She handed me an envelope. "This is an early payment, but I want those taxes paid."

She stood, and I nodded. "Thanks, sweetie." I placed the envelope in my pocket. "I'll catch up on my rest, and then we can make plans. I really want to help with the clinic."

Ginnie leaned down and embraced me. "Best friend, you take care of yourself." She gave a watery smile. "I don't know what I'd do without you." She waved at Seth and left.

"I think I'll soak in the tub and go to bed, honey." I rose from the sofa, rubbing my back and hip. "I'm about worn out."

"Too worn out for one more visitor?" Seth looked out the front window.

I peered around his shoulder. Franklin's truck pulled into the driveway. "Well, maybe just one more visitor."

Seth chuckled. "I'll wash dishes. Why don't you go sit on the porch for a bit and catch the evening breeze?"

I smiled at my hunk of a son and did just that. Franklin shot out of the cab of his truck and took the porch steps in a leap. "Belle." He clutched me to his chest. "Kevin told me what went on." He held me at arm's length and gazed into my eyes. "I set you up for this." He shook his head. "I had no idea how much danger you were in. I'm so sorry. I should've told Kevin right away."

I grabbed his forearm and squeezed. "Franklin, none of us had any way of knowing Darren and Charlie were involved. I made some stupid decisions and got embroiled in a fight that shouldn't have been mine." I smiled. "But in spite of it all, I'm safe and sound because God is faithful."

Franklin drew me to his chest once again, his chin resting on my head. That little nook on my cranium Seth always propped upon seemed to fit him, too. I listened to his heartbeat and inhaled his fragrance. The rough denim shirt caressed my cheek.

Thank You, Lord, for Your protection and for this precious moment.

I slid my arms around his waist and held on. What a good feeling. In a moment, he cupped my cheek with his hand and tilted my face to his. I gazed into those coffee-and-cream eyes surrounded by smile crinkles. His peppermint breath grazed my lips as he gently kissed me.

I stood on tiptoe and slid my arm around his neck. Pulling him closer, I returned his kiss full force. I'd nearly tasted death, and now I needed to taste life.

Umm, umm. It tasted mighty good.

24

Don made short work of my testimony. He asked for a play-by-play of the events and noted everything. Joe had a record stretching back some years and would do prison time. Charlie had been arrested for marijuana distribution before.

"Ginnie didn't know about his prior arrest?" Deputy Don flipped a page of his notebook and skimmed some questions, tipped his head, and searched my eyes.

"Not to my knowledge."

"Well, if she's going to have expensive dogs in her care, she'll need to screen applicants more carefully." He stood and tossed his notebook on the desk. "I think I'll talk to her about the whole hiring process."

"That would be wonderful, Don. She'd appreciate the help, I know." My eyes filled. "I'm grateful to you."

"We're all grateful, Aunt Belle." I looked at my nephew seated in the chair beside me. He'd driven over to talk with the sheriff and stayed while they interviewed me.

I reached up and gripped Don's meaty hand. "I can't thank you enough, dear friend." Moisture clouded my vision.

Don ducked his head, red creeping up over his uniform's collar. "Just doing my job, Belle. Just doing my job."

"You did a mighty fine one, in my opinion."

Kevin stood when I did, and his arms enveloped

me. "Thank God, you're safe, Aunt Belle," he whispered. He held me at arm's length. "What would the family be without Aunt Belle?"

"Boring? Able to focus on real police work?" I raised an eyebrow in Don's direction.

Both men laughed, and Kevin kissed my cheek. "Go home and rest." He propelled me toward the door. "You deserve a vacation."

~

I parked in front of the newly built two-story redbrick house and tried to breathe. My stomach knotted and queasiness began. *Simmons* was printed on the black mailbox. With one hand covering my heart, I opened the Jeep door and slid out. I straightened my skirt, took a deep gulp of air, and marched up the sidewalk, wondering if my sister-in-law was home.

Phoebe's surprised face reddened when she saw me. "Belle?"

"May I come in?" I choked out. I heard people talking inside. "Or is this a bad time?"

"My parents are visiting."

I closed my eyes, my mouth tugging into a smile. *Thank You, Lord; they're all here.* "Do you think they'd see me?"

She shrugged, pushed the door open wider, and ushered me in. I followed her down a short parquet-covered hall to a floral-draped dining room where Peter's family was gathered around the long table. My eyes scanned the familiar faces: Mrs. Blevins, Mr. B, Phoebe's husband, James, cousin Nicole, and her baby.

Phoebe stepped beside me. "We have company." All eyes looked our way. Mrs. Blevins gasped, and Peter's dad stood.

"Belle," he said. With two long strides he stepped to my side and crushed me in his arms. "How are you, dear?"

I nuzzled the familiar chin and inhaled his presence. Tears stung my eyes. I squinted, but some tears slid out, wetting his shirt. "I'm fine, Mr. B," I whispered.

He released me and held me at arm's length. "I think you are." He faced his wife. "Marsha, Belle's here." The statement was almost a command.

Mrs. Blevins blinked and tightened her grip on a napkin. "So I see." She flicked a glance at her husband and then spoke, "Is Seth with you?"

"No, he's not." My lips quivered. "I needed to speak to each of you. I'm so glad you're together."

Phoebe pointed to an empty chair next to James. "Would you like to join us?" The forced politeness in her tone stung.

I shook my head. "No, I'll only be a minute." I smiled at her. "But thank you for asking." I gripped the back of a chair. "I don't want to make this a dramatic speech, but I've come to ask your forgiveness."

Mrs. Blevins dropped her napkin, her eyes piercing mine. "Well, it's about time."

"Marsha," her husband growled. "Enough. Let Belle have her say."

I lowered my gaze to my white knuckles and took another deep breath. "I was very angry when Peter left.

I was angry at him and angry at all of you." I leveled a gaze at each one, allowing my words to hang in the air. "His betrayal seemed mirrored by yours. I not only lost a husband; I lost a family." My lips trembled, and I clenched my fist against my stomach.

Mrs. Blevins started to rise, but Mr. B put his hand on her arm. "Go on," he said.

"I'd been part of this clan for so many years, and suddenly there was no room for me." A lone tear trickled down my cheek. "I found myself jealous when you'd pick up Seth and not me. He got Christmas and birthday presents, but not me." A sob caught in my throat. "At church when someone's spouse dies, they get a casserole and comfort. When you get divorced, you get cast out and blamed. Especially if you're the preacher's wife." I peeked at Mr. B and saw tears glisten in his eyes. "I know you had your emotions to deal with after Peter's betrayal."

Phoebe sucked in air. "Don't start. . . ."

Again Mr. Blevins came to my rescue. "Phoebe, we owe it to Belle to let her speak."

"I don't owe her anything," Phoebe sniped.

"No, Phoebe, you don't," I said. "I owe you something. I owe you my forgiveness. What you do with it is your business. But I don't want to harbor resentment and bitterness against this family for another moment." I shuddered. "I've had a very upsetting experience in the last few days, and God and I've had plenty of time to talk. And we decided I had to face each of you and say I forgive you." Exhausted, I stopped.

The room echoed in silence. Finally Mr. Blevins

spoke. "Belle, I accept your forgiveness and ask you to forgive me."

I smiled. I could see weary lines around his eyes. "Thank you, sir."

No one else spoke.

I tugged my purse strap to my shoulder, about to leave. "Well, it was nice to see you. I hope you're doing well. I'll tell Seth to give you a call."

"Belle, wait." Mrs. Blevins slid out of her chair. She reached my side in a few quick steps, her chubby arms extended, and I stepped into her embrace. "I'm sorry, dear." She sobbed against my hair. "I just couldn't face what he did to all of us. I am sorry I treated you badly." I held her tightly and let her cry, tears coursing down my cheeks, too. "My boy was so wrong, and I couldn't face what he'd done. He was so wrong."

"Thank you," I whispered into her gray hair. "Thank you for many happy years and for my wonderful son." I pushed her back to gaze into her eyes. "For if you hadn't had Peter, I wouldn't have my Seth." I kissed her forehead.

Mrs. Blevins pointed to the empty chair. "I have your favorite chocolate cola cake. Won't you join us?"

I glanced at Phoebe, who stood frozen, arms at her sides, her mouth in a grim line. "I really need to go rest. But thank you." I felt my lips tip in a smile. "I still need to get your recipe, that family secret stuff."

Mrs. Blevins laughed. "I'll mail it to you this next week, dear." Her face brightened. "Or would it be possible for me to come to your new house and drop a cake off with the recipe?"

The white flag had been waved and accepted by

most. My ex-mother-in-law was struggling to make amends. And if she wanted to use chocolate to salve the wound, so be it. "That would be wonderful." I flicked a glance at my sister-in-law. "Phoebe has my new number." Her posture hadn't changed a whit. I reckoned we would have to fight our battle another day. For now, Peter's parents would do.

I'm sure the sun was brighter when I started toward my car, and I know my heart was lighter. Forgiveness. A scouring pad for the heart.

Just as I was about to pull away, Seth drove up. He sprinted to my window. "What on earth are you doing here?"

"Hello to you, too."

He stammered, "I mean, why. . . ? Aunt Phoebe's. . . Did you know. . . ?"

I laughed. "Did I know your grandmother has chocolate cola cake? Yes, but I'm afraid I'll have to wait to get a piece." I reached out the window and stroked his cheek. "Things are looking up in the Blevins family, son. I just had a short visit, and things went well. Really well."

He gripped my hand. "Oh, Mom. I'm so glad. It's been too awkward for years."

I chuckled. "That's putting it mildly." I shifted into drive. "Go get some cake before your cousin gobbles it up. We'll talk later. I love you."

He leaned in and pecked my cheek. "Arabelle Blevins, I'm so glad you're my mom." Rocking back on his heels, he added, "But go straight home. No more trouble for you, young lady."

Shaking my head and laughing, I drove toward my wonderful, paint peeled, old house.

25

The first Saturday morning in June, Ginnie held her open house at the Pampered Pooch. She showcased the place. We had decorated with every doggie balloon and streamer in the Jackson-Trennan area. A huge chocolate cola cake in the shape of a dog tag sat in the foyer. A sign read, "Keep Your Pet Safe." On a knee-high table was a bowl of pepperoni bits compliments of the Pet Deli. People and pups milled in and out all morning long for guided tours.

"Belle, this had to be the best idea ever." Ginnie's long, flowing red skirt caught in the breeze. "Thank you again for finding diamonds in the dust." She grabbed my arm. "The bank called, and the loan went through."

"Hallelujah." We high-fived and hugged. Parceling off one and a half acres of land and two old redbrick houses to Ginnie plumped up my savings account and would allow me to keep taxes paid on the rest of the property for a good long while.

She peered into my eyes. "How are you feeling?"

"I'm doing well, thanks." And I was. Despite the first two nights of clinging fear, I had improved. Seth insisted on staying with me for the first few days, but he'd gone home after a while, and life returned to normal. I still slept with the bathroom light on, but no one knew that but God and me. Nightmares of spiders and cellars had about dissipated, thank goodness.

"Mrs. Reynolds?" a woman called.

Ginnie whirled, "Be right there." She faced me. "I'm signing up more day camp customers." She giggled and fairly skipped in the lady's direction.

I laughed. After learning about the alarming rate that dogs disappeared, doggie daycare didn't seem foolish after all.

By two o'clock, folks appeared on the front lawn under a red-and-white striped tent for lemonade, chocolate chip cookies, and doggie biscuits to hear Dr. Carlton speak on responsible pet ownership. Ginnie stood by his side, interjecting ideas and helping him field questions. His warm smile in her direction caught my attention. Then she batted her eyelashes a time or two. I glanced at his left hand. No ring. Stifling a laugh, I left the tent. Poor Glenn Higgs. Looked like he had missed his chance.

I sauntered through the grounds. Donetta Robbins fluttered her fingers in my direction, an elaborate diamond ring glittering in the sunshine. "Did you get your raffle ticket for the handmade quilt?" She was in her fund-raising element after recruiting several craft organizations and local businesses for donations to raise money for the Jackson pet shelter.

I fluttered my fingers back. "I surely did. Thanks." I didn't even grit my teeth.

John Clarence passed out pamphlets from the vet containing coupons for regular checkups and vaccinations, his brother nowhere in sight. Linda Lester hosted a table presenting information on ID microchipping, with Schotzie as her demo model. Linda told Schotzie's rescue story over and over. Seth's photographer snapped their picture for a front-page story, I was sure. Violet's pet health insurance agent scooted about the crowd.

After Dr. Carlton's spiel, more people wanted a guided tour. I stepped forward to take the first names on the list. Mel and Belinda? I turned and saw Belinda holding Mustard's leash and waved them over.

"I had no idea you were coming today." I glanced toward the building to see if Ginnie was in sight.

Mel must've caught my look. "Honey, go on in, get out of the heat. I'll be right there." Belinda beamed a smile and tugged her beagle toward the kennel. "Belle, I acted right foolish around here, and I owe Ginnie an apology. Think she'll take me up on it?"

"You'd best ask her, Mel."

He shuffled and ran his hand over his jaw. "I've not been the best husband to my bride, but I'm trying to change. We've been to some counseling sessions at the church."

I brightened. "Well, I'll be praying for you."

"Please do." He started to leave then stopped. "There's no fool like an old fool, but this fool wants to learn to live the right way."

"I'm truly glad to hear that, Mel. Truly glad." He smiled and followed Belinda.

A couple new to the area were next on the tour waiting list. I motioned for them to follow when someone called my name. I turned to see Lauren Cooper trotting up the walk.

"Mrs. Blevins, I thought that was you." She slung an arm about my shoulders. "How good to see you."

"Lauren." I squeezed her waist. "Did you bring a doggie to the fair?"

We both laughed. "Actually, not today. I will, but my main girl is getting ready to whelp, and I didn't want to take any chances."

I smiled. "Mommies know best."

She grinned and looked around. "Um, so you are helping Mrs. Reynolds out today?"

"Yes, I'm a hostess." I glanced down at the smock I wore. "Don't I look all pet involved?"

Her airy laugh made me grin. "You do, indeed." She glanced behind me. "I see a photographer. Is he from the paper?"

A smile tipped my lips. "Yes, that's the photographer from the *Jackson News.*" I grasped her elbow. "Hang on just a minute, Lauren." I spoke to the couple about to take the tour. "Would you mind continuing without me for just a second?" They walked down the first hall and rummaged through a stack of chew toys on a table.

"You won't believe what all is on display out back. Maybe you'd like to see the area." I lifted an eyebrow.

Her eyes twinkled. "Why, I might be interested."

"How's your family?" Gravel crunched as we walked toward the tents set up near the pasture.

Lauren's hand flitted in the air. "Mom and Dad are doing well. I'm teaching in Jackson now, so my family consists of first graders." She laughed. "And Chihuahuas."

"Still single, then?"

Her giggle made me smile. "Still single. Until the Lord finds me the right guy, I'll stay single."

We walked behind the kennel. Under a striped awning, a massage table was set up, and a poodle enjoyed kneading by a local masseuse. Seth talked to the man as he worked.

"Son," I said.

Seth glanced our way then stopped, a perfect white smile softening his features. "Hi, Lauren."

"I have a couple to tour through the kennel area. Would you be able to answer questions for Lauren?" I blinked innocently.

Seth's blue eyes gleamed. He slid his hand in his pocket and pulled out a peppermint. "Here, Mother. I thought I had a Tootsie Roll, but I don't." He handed me the candy and took Lauren's hand. "Come see this massage deal, Lauren. I think I might be the next customer."

I backed away, unwrapping the candy and popping it in my mouth. I stood to watch the pair. *They'd have such cute kids, Lord, I know they would.*

"Cute couple," Franklin said as he approached. He slid one arm about my waist. "Do we know her?"

"We do." I smiled into his eyes. "We like her a lot. She's a dog show enthusiast, too."

"Then she can't be all bad." He smiled. "You through for the day?" His fingers intertwined with mine, and he gave me a gentle kiss. "I like peppermint," he whispered against my lips.

I squeezed his hand. "I have one couple waiting for a tour inside, and then I think I'm finished."

He placed his forehead against mine. "How about dinner?"

"Sounds good." I smiled. "Grady's?"

He hugged me closer, his breath lifting my bangs. "How about a T-bone steak with Buster, Sadie, and me?"

"You cooking? Sounds like an offer I can't refuse."

"Of course my house is a bit untidy."

"Franklin Jeffries"—my tone rose, and I propped my hands on my hips—"I'm not going to clean your house. I'm going for dinner and that's all."

"No white-gloved inspections?"

"Not even one, I promise."

"Good, because the mulch I ordered for your front flower bed hasn't arrived." He grinned. "Guess our bartering will start next week."

"Mowing for feather dusting? Sounds like a good deal to me." We started toward the kennel, and my gaze roved over the pasture. I wondered if Franklin would like living in the country.

Hand in hand, we wandered into the Pampered Pooch.

Eileen Key, a retired teacher, taught middle school for thirty years and survived. She is now a freelance writer and editor. She has published eight anthology stories and numerous articles and devotionals. *Dog Gone* is her first novel. A lifelong reader, Eileen has owned library cards from eight different cities. Eileen is an active member of Grace Community Church. Keeping up with her three grown children and their families is her delight. Any spare time is devoted to two amazing grandkids. Visit her Web site at www.eileenkey.com

You may correspond with this author by writing:
Eileen Key
Author Relations
PO Box 721
Uhrichsville, OH 44683

A Letter to Our Readers

Dear Reader:
In order to help us satisfy your quest for more great mystery stories, we would appreciate it if you would take a few minutes to respond to the following questions. We welcome your comments and read each form and letter we receive. When completed, please return to:

Fiction Editor
Heartsong Presents—MYSTERIES!
PO Box 721
Uhrichsville, Ohio 44683

Did you enjoy reading *Dog Gone* by Eileen Key?

⚲ Very much! I would like to see more books like this!
The one thing I particularly enjoyed about this story was:

_____
_____
_____

⚲ Moderately. I would have enjoyed it more if:

_____
_____
_____

Are you a member of the HP—MYSTERIES! Book Club?
⚲ Yes ⚲ No

If no, where did you purchase this book?

_____

Please rate the following elements using a scale of 1 (poor) to 10 (superior):

___ Main character/sleuth   ___ Romance elements

___ Inspirational theme   ___ Secondary characters

___ Setting   ___ Mystery plot

How would you rate the cover design on a scale of 1 (poor) to 5 (superior)? _____

What themes/settings would you like to see in future **Heartsong Presents—MYSTERIES!** selections? _____
_____
_____
_____

Please check your age range:
- ◯ Under 18   ◯ 18–24
- ◯ 25–34   ◯ 35–45
- ◯ 46–55   ◯ Over 55

Name: _____

Occupation: _____

Address: _____

E-mail address: _____